INDIGARA

Books by Tanith Lee

The Birthgrave Trilogy
The Birthgrave
Vazkor, Son of Vazkor
Quest for the White Witch

The Blood Opera Sequence
Dark Dance
Personal Darkness
Darkness, I
Scarabseque,
The Girl Who Broke Dracula

The Claidi Journals
Wolf Tower
Wolf Star
Wolf Queen
Wolf Wing

The Elaidh Stories
Girls in Green Dresses
The Sea Was in Her Eyes

The Four-BEE Series
Don't Bite the Sun
Drinking Sapphire Wine

The Jaisel Stories
Northern Chess
Southern Lights

The Journals of St. Strange
The Story Told by Smoke
Old Flame

The Lionwolf Trilogy
Cast a Bright Shadow
Here in Cold Hell
No Flame But Mine

The Novels of Vis
The Storm Lord
Anackire
The White Serpent

The Piratica Books
Piratica
Piratica II: *Return to Parrot Island*
Piratica III: *The Family Sea*

The Secret Books of Paradys
The Book of the Damned
The Book of the Beast
The Book of the Dead
The Book of the Mad
Doll Skulls

The Secret Books of Venus
Faces Under Water
Saint Fire
A Bed of Earth
Venus Preserved

The S.I.L.V.E.R. Series
The Silver Metal Lover
Metallic Love

FIREBIRD
WHERE SCIENCE FICTION SOARS™

INDIGARA

OR, JET AND OTIS CONQUER THE WORLD

TANITH LEE

FIREBIRD

AN IMPRINT OF PENGUIN GROUP (USA) INC.

FIREBIRD
Published by the Penguin Group
Penguin Group (USA) Inc., 345 Hudson Street, New York, New York 10014, U.S.A.
Penguin Group (Canada), 90 Eglinton Avenue East, Suite 700, Toronto, Ontario, Canada M4P 2Y3
(a division of Pearson Penguin Canada Inc.)
Penguin Books Ltd, 80 Strand, London WC2R 0RL, England
Penguin Ireland, 25 St Stephen's Green, Dublin 2, Ireland
(a division of Penguin Books Ltd)
Penguin Group (Australia), 250 Camberwell Road, Camberwell, Victoria 3124, Australia
(a division of Pearson Australia Group Pty Ltd)
Penguin Books India Pvt Ltd, 11 Community Center, Panchsheel Park,
New Delhi - 110 017, India
Penguin Group (NZ), 67 Apollo Drive, Rosedale, North Shore 0632,
New Zealand (a division of Pearson New Zealand Ltd)
Penguin Books (South Africa) (Pty) Ltd, 24 Sturdee Avenue,
Rosebank, Johannesburg 2196, South Africa

Registered Offices: Penguin Books Ltd, 80 Strand, London WC2R 0RL, England

Published by Firebird, an imprint of Penguin Group (USA) Inc., 2007

1 3 5 7 9 10 8 6 4 2

Text copyright © Tanith Lee, 2007

THE LIBRARY OF CONGRESS CATALOGING-IN-PUBLICATION DATA
Lee, Tanith.
Indigara / by Tanith Lee.
p. cm. Summary: When her annoying older sister gets a bit part in a movie,
fourteen-year-old Jet and her family travel to Ollywood—the movie capital of their earth-like
planet—where, on a trip through the city's subways, Jet and her robot dog Otis are transported
to a world of rejected fantasy and science fiction movies and must try to find their way back to reality.

[1. Motion picture industry—Fiction. 2. Diaries—Fiction. 3. Science fiction. 4. Fantasy.] I. Title.
PZ7.L5149In 2007
[Fic]—dc22
2007014463

ISBN 978-0-14-240922-0

Printed in the United States of America

In memory of all those wonderful pilot movies that never became series.

And with endless thanks to John Kaiine for the scenario, and Shostakovich and Holst for the music—Shostakovich's Symphony No. 1, the second movement; Holst's ballet from *The Perfect Fool*

Up many and many a marvellous shrine
Whose wreathéd friezes intertwine
The viol, the violet, and the vine.
—"The City in the Sea," Edgar Allan Poe

PART ONE

OTIS'S DISKRIPT

The problem was that on that day I was supposed to go in for my half-yearly service appointment.

The company, S.C. Deluxe, had smailed the Latters. But at the last moment, of course, Turquoise's role was confirmed in the top-budget movie *Fall of Super Troy*. There was no way at all that the parental Latters would miss taking Turquoise and her sisters to Ollywood. And so my appointment was canceled. Naturally all Simulate Canine products are guaranteed for each full year, even if a single service is missed. It should, however, preferably *not* be missed. Tiny things can go wrong, as S.C. Deluxe's manual informs all proud owners of a robot dog. But, as so often happens, the Latters had only skimmed the manual, and it goes without saying no one consulted *me*.

Instead, everything was gotten ready in a rush, and two days after, we were all aboard transocean flight 701 XY. Though I, of course, traveled in a crate in the hold.

Jet's Journal

One day I'm going to kill Turquoise. I'll boil her in honey and spread her on the front lawn. Or I'll drown her in a vat of warm bottled water and her most expensive shampoo. Or—

Or maybe I'll kill Amber first.

Yes. That's the best idea.

Save Amber from herself.

Because Amber is already awful, and in another year or so Amber is going to be just as bad—unbelievable, but a fact—or worse. Than Turquoise.

Basically Turquoise is eighteen and Amber is sixteen.

People seem to change at about sixteen. Or *they* both did. Though I actually don't mean people, I mean sisters. Mine.

I am fourteen, and when *I* was ten and Amber was twelve and *Turquoise* was fourteen, we were all fine, or so I thought. Then one day Turquoise turned into a bitch on wheels, and Amber, who was fourteen, and I, who was twelve, said, *What has gotten into that damn Turquoise?* This day was, in fact, about two months after Turquoise's sixteenth birthday, when we all went to Dazzleland. And since then Turquoise has gone from worse to worstest. But meanwhile Amber became sixteen, and on her very birthday I thought, *What has gotten into that damn Amber? She is a bitch on wheels.*

Sometimes I wonder if it will happen to me when I'm sixteen. But if it does, there'll be only me to wonder what's gotten into that damn Jet, who will then be a b-on-w.

No, I don't think it'll happen to me.

I'm not like them at all.

I mean, Turquoise is tall and curvy and has long, long blond hair and huge blue (turquoise, you see) eyes. And Amber is tall and more curvy and has blue eyes and red (amber, you see) hair.

And Jet (me) is short and skinny and has wiry very black (yeah, you guessed it, jet black) hair and (jet black)

3

eyes. And while my sisters are, I have grudgingly to admit, stunning to look at, I am nothing to look at—as I have very recently found out for sure, when not only Georgis Hann but also my backup possibility, Scott Paperley, ignored me, both in class and out of class, all year. Also I'm not (apparently) Artistic, like Turquoise, or (apparently) Unusual, like Amber. I just am. I mean, I'm just alive and getting on with living.

Which is, frankly, more than enough to cope with.

Sometimes I think of the old story of Cinderella, in a new form. There is the one poor Ugly Sister, jet black Cinder-hairy, bullied and lorded over by the two horrible Beautiful Sisters, and if anyone's going to the Ball, it isn't going to be Cinder-hairy. Anyway, you wouldn't catch me in a glass slipper. Not with my big feet.

I suppose you could say the Ball happened for Turquoise, at least, last Fiveday, when the smail came in that said she'd landed the part in the movie *FOST.*

Oh, the scenes. She cried for joy and so did Mom and Dad, and so did Amber. But then *she* got jealous and cried *without* joy in the downstairs bathroom with the shower running so no one could hear her sniffling—*I want it—I want to be in movies*—only I did hear.

And what did I do? Nothing.

And in the end Mom said to me, "Honey, aren't you pleased Turquoise is going to play Helenet's Third Damsel in *Fall of Super Troy*?"

And I said, "Sure."

And Amber, just out of the shower, said, "My eyes are red because soap went in them, but Jet's just a jealous, nasty little kid. Everything always has to be about *her*."

"Sure," I said. "I'm really jealous. I'd rather be eaten alive by a crocodile with blunt teeth than play Third Damsel to Helenet."

And Mom said, "Oh, girls."

And Dad said, "Just going for a round of golf."

And Mom said, "Only think, Jet, we're all going to fly out to Ollywood. Now isn't that exciting?"

"Sure," I said.

Is it?

Exciting?

I mean, maybe it is.

5

Only I know how it'll go.

It'll be *Turquoise* this and *Turquoise* that and *don't upset Turquoise* and *nobody make a noise because Turquoise* is *learning her lines with her electro learn-a-lot*, and *now we must go to this showbiz party that will last until seven the next morning earthclocktime*, and where everyone will be all over Turquoise and perhaps Amber, and Mom and Dad will drink champagne Sec (or Sick, as I call it) and get giggly and hold hands or dance together to some old, ancient music by Coldplay or Eminem, and no one will say a word to me and I will be so completely glad they don't as I will have died, due to boredom or Mom-Dad embarrassment.

But I guess it's exciting.

Ollywood is the movie capital on Planet Obelisk.

It's called after some long-ago old actor. Horrel Lardy, I think was his other name. And he was two people. No, that's not right . . .

Anyhow it's now one in the morning, earthclocktime. And I have my last class in school tomorrow. Where Georgis and Scott can really ignore me properly before this semester ends.

Night, all. Night, Otis.

(I like Otis. He switches off circuits at night to pretend he's asleep.)

Otis is a gentleman. Even if he's a dog. (His fur, in this low light, is all tufted and silvery.) A robot dog, Deluxe.

STUDIOCITY: OVERVIEW

Flight 701 XY lands with a slight bump, for which the robo-pilot apologizes. Apparently there is a flood of weed-guano on the runway. Since weed-guano can spring up inside of five minutes, despite the wonders of technology, no one can ever quite get ahead of it.

A polished, nine-seater slinkousine picks the Latters up from the airport. They are by now escorted by two execs and one producer's assistant from the studios.

But there has already been a press rush.

Turquoise has been cameradioed for twenty minutes, posing this way, now that, speaking of how happy she is to have been chosen for Third Damsel. An exec finally detaches Turquoise, and she and everyone else are whisked away in the slinko to their hotel in Studiocity. Their luggage follows in another vehicle. Otis, still in his crate, is included with this, but in the trunk.

Studiocity lies behind seventy-foot-wide, two-hundred-

TANITH LEE

foot-high gates of platinebony, under red banners that carry in gold the Studiocity logo: DREAM-SPINNERS TO THE PLANET.

Desert palms and forest cedars also tower hundreds of feet high along the broad white Avenue of Fame and Fortune. Classical-looking buildings soar on all sides. The perfect weather-controlled sky is the deepest blue.

Then the hotel building appears.

It is shaped like a gigantic white swan.

High on the vast curved neck, two golden eyes in the swan's head are the windows of a colossal banquet-ballroom.

"Oh," says Turquoise.

"Ohh," says Amber.

Mom murmurs to Jet, "Look at *that*, honey."

Jet says, "Oh sure. The duck."

OTIS'S DISKRIPT

Unfortunately, the Latter house robot had not packed me very well. Had I not been switched off for the journey, I could have put this right, but Mr. Latter had insisted I switch off *before* packing. He gets nervous about all property.

The result of the mistake was that no sooner did my auto-system wake me in the hotel, switch me back on, and I stood up, than my left hind leg fell off.

I was forced to spend several minutes trying to make the in-apartment robot understand what was needed. The machine seemed to believe I was human and so called a medic. Then it became certain I was an animal-dog and called a vet. Just after the proper maintenance had arrived, and my leg was being put right, two men with a stretcher burst in, soon followed by the vet.

Luckily the Latters had all gone to have brunch with some studio people.

Once I had explained, the medics laughed and went. The vet was harder to get rid of.

He was still there when Jet reappeared unexpectedly. She managed to get him to leave, though he then seemed of the opinion I was an animal and Jet was the robot. I assumed he was insane. Jet flung herself on a couch.

I sat down and looked at her attentively, the way she likes. I even put on the little soft glow light in my eyes. She seemed very unhappy.

"Guess what they wanted for brunch—those awful execs and Turquoise—even Mom and Dad. Pan-fried dashcashy. Oh, and Amber had swamp-wasp pâté."

"That is bad?"

"*Very* bad. I had eggs earthside-up and a muffin. Then I said I was tired."

She sighed.

I went over and jumped up beside her, and she leaned on me.

"There'll be at least three months of this," she said. "At home even school stops for the weekend. So that's just six days of hell and then three days off for—well, only home-hell."

We gazed together from the window at the tops of pines. A faint trail of weather-controlled fluffy clouds was passing overhead. Red and gold smoke-writing swirled over, too, reading: OLLYWOOD, CAPITAL OF DREAMS.

But already I could see a little patch of weed-guano growing by the edge of the window. I correctly predicted that, by the time the hotel systems were alerted and crawled out to it, it would be the size of a soccer ball.

SETTLING IN: MONTAGE

Prefilming began on Oneday.

Turquoise's personal exec took charge of her, and Turquoise, who was already installed in her own separate hotel, began to turn into a remote other being, nothing much to do with her family anymore.

She *became* the Third Damsel, whose name was Ariasta.

Turquoise, when or if they met for lunch or dinner, had been swallowed by her role.

"*He* says we must *live* our parts. On set *or* off. At all times."

Dad was all over the place with pride, horror, and grief, when Turquoise-Ariasta would eat only ash-plums for lunch, and drink only red grape juice with a spoonful of Rise-and-Shine in it. Also because she came to meals if not in costume, then in costume-type floaty robes, her eyes all full of Ollywood dreams, whispering her lines of (stilted sounding) dialogue to the bread and butter.

"*He* says nothing matters but the movie. Until the movie is done, we belong to it. And to *him*."

"*Does* he?" said Dad. "This guy—"

"Hush, honey," said Mom in her briskly gentle not-now-dear voice.

He, the *guy*—one of the most famous directors of modern Ollywood—specialized in the Epic Picture. He had made *Son of Beowulf Unchained* and *Building Rome in a Day*. His name was Rector Pandion, but everyone, Turquoise had told them, called him Reck. Because he was "reckless," a risk taker, and would try anything in his work for the sake of Art.

Turquoise, though, had begun to look even lovelier than usual. The now daily routine of steam baths, massage, facials, makeup, and hairstyling, perhaps even the steady diet of plums and juice and Rise-and-Shine, made her *gleam*.

"The sheen on her hair," Jet remarked to Otis, "blinds you. You need to put on shades to look at her. Not," she added, "that I do, much."

Amber sulked. She, too, went on a diet—asparagus. She, too, went to Studiocity's baths and massages, and to exercise classes. She had an exercise bike brought to the family's rooms in the hotel, and spent two hours a day pedaling on it noisily.

"She's like a hamster on a hamster wheel," said Jet.

Mom and Dad, apart from Dad's worries over Reck, grew young, silly, and carefree. They swam and went dancing. They were often out late. Jet felt like a parent. She frowned when they didn't come in until dawn and then slept in till noon.

Jet and Otis walked the wide avenues of Studiocity—the Avenue of Award-Winning Stars, the Avenue of Fame Forever. They found a park and ran races, Otis tactfully letting Jet win one race in three—which she knew, but tactfully pretended she didn't.

"Jet's big feet are getting even bigger," said Amber. "It's all that walking and running. You're not eleven *now*, Jetty. Haven't you heard of exercise classes, in school?"

"Your butt has gotten bigger, too," said Jet thoughtfully. "Maybe it's from sitting on that bike."

Amber screamed.

Next day Reck invited Dad for a drink in some glass bubble of office miles up in some building, and Dad came back saying what a great guy Reck was after all.

Turquoise now made everyone play parts at dinner. "I mean, not parts actually in the movie. But so I can go on getting in the right mood for Ariasta. Perhaps you could all act lesser servants. Yes, that's it."

All through the meal, if she spoke to any of them, it was an order: "Fetch me that salt hither, slave."

Mom only beamed and passed the salt.

Not even Dad recoiled when Turquoise addressed him with "Fie, rodent, back to your hovel." To Amber, Turquoise said, "You shall be whipped." When Amber dared to join in this playact with: "Spare me, mighty Damsel," Turquoise returned to planet with a thump. "Oh, *don't* try and improvise, Amber, *please*. You don't know how to do it. And now you've spoiled my concentration."

To Jet, Turquoise said little or nothing. None of them now said much to Jet. Jet became invisible.

Jet's Journal
She has only fifteen lines in all.

I've counted them. I've had enough chance; all she does is say them over and over. Also I played back the learn-a-lot yesterday.

Fifteen lines. About fifty words.

Most of them are: *Yes, Lady.* Which she says to this

Helenet princess, who's in love with the hero whose name I forget—but he's played by Bronze Shunk, who Amber collapses at. He once walked through the restaurant. All the females swooned (even Mom looked weird). Not me. He's all muscles, but his face is too small, just like his eyes are. Well, I think so. But I suppose if you're eight feet tall as he is, your head and eyes are a long way off, so maybe they just look smaller. (I think Georgis Hann is better looking, even though he's only fifteen and ignores me.)

We've now been here three weeks; that's twenty-seven days. Sorry. Twenty-seven millennia.

Had a weird dream last night.

Dreamed the weed-guano was back on the window, but now it was deep blue and there were berries growing in it. And then a fish—that is, a FISH—swam through it.

And I could hear this musical sound, on and on, quite tuneful. It was like—what's it called—an oboe, that old instrument they still have in some orchestras. But you can't hear anything from outside through the glass, ever. And no one in our rooms had on a telecine, or music center.

And Amber wasn't even on her hamster bike. And all the soundstages here are soundproof anyway, inside and out.

I met this guy in the westside park. He's old, I guess about thirty or something. He was feeding the birds despite notices saying DON'T FEED THE BIRDS. So I sort of liked that.

Then he said he liked Otis.

Mom and Dad always say, *Don't talk to strangers.* They are completely right, and I don't, but sometimes you can just exchange a word or two, because otherwise it gets stupid.

So I said that yeah, Otis was good.

Then he asked was Otis an S.C. Deluxe, and although most sane people (unlike that insane hotel vet) realize Otis is a robot, few get the brand. I never mind as much if they make a comment as long as they recognize Otis is extra special.

When I agreed, the guy—whose name is Ben—said he'd known someone years back who'd had an S.C. Deluxe, and that one was pretty great, but Otis is fantastic.

So I let Otis go over, and then Ben just started talking

to him like you would with an intelligent person, and of course Otis can answer and is super intelligent, so they had this conversation. All about old movies of ten or so years ago. (Otis has memory files. I think he extended his one on film when he knew we were coming here.)

Ben told us he's a robo-warden in Studiocity's Subway, the below-surface streets and stores, and where the trains run. He has a gang of thirty robo-cleaners. He told me some stuff about things that happen down there. How you can sometimes hear a phantom train run through just after one in the morning. And people have seen "things," though he didn't say what they were.

But to me it all sounds more interesting than anything up here. Anyone can go down there. *We* haven't because the others only hang around the hotel—or are filming, and I didn't know. But I do now.

Ben says he's lost six robots from his gang during the nine years he's been working down there. That is, *lost*.

They just disappear, he said. He said a couple of people have, too. Had I ever heard of an actress called Rena Kimber? I hadn't. He said it was before he was here, about twenty years ago. There was a movie made in

Studiocity called *The Wicked Couple*, and Rena Kimber, an unknown actress, starred in it, but she'd gotten a bad reputation suddenly, and she threw a wild party in the Subway one night, and at about three in the morning they looked around and she had vanished. And later everywhere was searched, only they never found her. Not even her *body*.

Maybe he was trying to scare me.

Don't think so. Though he kind of looked at me real close, to see how I'd take it. Anyhow, I wasn't.

I asked why they need to use human workers to oversee the robot gangs—I've noticed they do that here. Ben says all the machinery goes wrong a lot. It's something to do, they say, with all the extra tech stuff they need for filming, the superputers and ultralectrics. So many machines they're making one another fuse. There're always things not working or shorting out.

Even Turquoise (who I am definitely going to kill soon—maybe I'll push Amber over on top of her and they'll both explode) said one of the huge Magni Overcameras on set superheated, and the whole lot had to be evacuated for twenty whole minutes and didn't poor old oogly Wreck get all stressy-wessy.

Anyway, maybe tomorrow, which is Earthday and first day of the weekend, I can escape with Otis to the Subway. Turquoise told us we're all supposed to be going to a picnic on the roof garden on top of Fame Palace tomorrow, and I truly want to miss that.

Night, Otis.

Love you, Otis. Silver fur, that's you, you smart old Deluxe. Loved the way you looked at Ben and said, "So nice to have met you."

And if he'd tried to shake your paw, which he didn't, I'd have shoved one of those birds he was feeding up his nose.

2

SUBWAY: OVERVIEW

By some called the Underworld, though it is not, Ollywood's Subway stretches for miles in all directions, beneath Studiocity, and beyond. It involves far more than underground trains.

Down here, too, are sidewalks and highways, though most of these are very narrow, and in some parts alleys branch off, running between the walls of small warehouses and stores, and under the arches of the highways or overhead tracks. The trains rumble along for twenty-one hours out of the earthclocktime twenty-four. But between

midnight and three in the morning all the tracks fall silent—apart, of course, from the odd ghost train said still
to run there. The reason for the three-hour stoppage has
to do with some outdated regulation that no one has ever
bothered to get changed. Busy stagehands and set build-
ers, trying to shift endless loads from soundstage to stage,
sometimes curse this ban.

The Subway is lit by huge high-up lamps, shaped like
elegant parasols of yellowish or mauvish glass.

Here and there are fake trees—orange, tulip, et cetera—and hanging baskets of fake flowers, while fake
creeper "grows" sometimes up the sides of buildings.

The trains are electric blue or vivid pumpkin.

The ones who designed the Subway did their very best
to make it colorful and bright. They perhaps succeeded
too well.

In many places enormous pipelike structures run down
through everything. They come in at the high roof above
(which is the floor or ground of Studiocity), passing on
down and away through the roads or ground of the Subway.
These pipes, many of which are as wide around as eighty
feet, are also cheerfully painted with scenes from old

classic Earth movies—*Great Expectations* (in color), *Star Wars*, *Lord of the Rings*—*1*, *2*, and *3*, or *Nightmare on Elm Street*.

Elevators run up and down inside some of these pipe structures. Several are for the use of people descending from or returning to Studiocity. But most serve the mechanical needs of the soundstages and the imaging studios—way down, below even the Subway, is the true Underworld of Ollywood.

There lie the vast warehouses of props and fully dressed sets—small, large, and gigantic: Ancient Rome, Egypt, Greece, Europe, and America—or as much of them as Ollywood has, over the years, re-created—lurk in unlit shadowy vaults, kept stable, often in subzero temperatures. And alongside lie the libraries of archaic celluloid film, of computer graphics and IT Supremistics. Even of old, tattered scripts on paper, these last locked safe in transparent vacuum boxes.

Although sometimes new directors look at such relics—usually only via superputer link upstairs—mostly this place is like an old attic, built the wrong way around in the basement. You don't always want to throw everything away. It may have some funny old sentimental value. But then again, you're not really that interested in it anymore.

So there it lies, in the upside-down attic of Ollywood's Underworld.

Quietly rotting and no doubt falling apart.

OTIS'S DISKRIPT

Jet is, in her way, a sensible young woman, and she is careful about to whom she talks. But she forgets, because she often pretends to forget, that I have fully operational sensors that can tell if the other human in question is someone reasonable, or one she should avoid.

So I'd known at once that the man in the park, the robo-warden, Ben, was perfectly all right. A bit empty, with a sort of shadowy personality, as if he wasn't quite there, it is true. But some humans have unhappy lives. They lose their spark.

And then, too, I am there to guard Jet. Mr. Latter, though often foolish, is still not quite a fool.

Jet's Journal

I told them I didn't want to go on the roof picnic.

Everyone was *so* concerned.

Even Turquoise, to my horrified amazedness, swayed in and said, "But J, *Bronze* is going to be there."

"Who?" I asked.

Turquoise narrowed her namesake eyes. "Jet, you can be such a little ignorant jerk."

I blinked. I said, "No, *that's* impossible, Turkey." (I call her Turkey sometimes. Have done so ever since she was sixteen and became a b-on-w.)

She flung out.

I mean, really *flung* herself.

Which meant her flimsy draperies got caught on something by the door, and there was a piercing wail—*Oh, my best dress is all torn, and it's all Jet's fault*, and on and on.

Then in came Mom, and I said I had a headache. And she agreed I should stay at the hotel and just call the robo-service if I needed anything.

Amber looked in, too, just before they finally left.

"Too cluck-cluck chicken to go, huh, brat? Scared Bronze won't even look at you, like he would anyhow? Stupid little dope."

I yawned.

24

If Bronze Shunk looked at me on purpose, I'd throw up. On his Trojan sandals if I could manage it.

The elevator to the Subway was packed going down.

There are a lot of stores and diners down there, and only a few rich-people-only ones in Studiocity.

I was pleased to find all the crowd was ordinary folk, like yours truly, Jet Latter.

It felt like a real weekend.

Exec girls chattering about buying shoes and who they were dating tonight in which Subway restaurant, and girls and guys arguing about scripts they were working on—writers are usually not that important, and not the ones with any spare stollars. Some little kids bounced about wanting to buy toys and Kongburgers, or just to ride the trains. Some tech people live with their families in Ollywood, too.

We all stepped out on Sunset Boulevard, which is one of the wider Subway streets.

Otis and I spent some time watching the blue and tangerine trains speeding along the track below.

Ben had told me about the big pipes that run up and

down between Studiocity and the Subway, and then on down to the storage areas. And he'd told me some of the creepy stories about ghost trains and vanishing people: Rena Kimber, and some man Ben didn't name.

I wandered around and did some store-gazing, then went in a diner for a soda.

It wasn't too busy. I sat at the counter and after a while I asked the human waitress—who was taking the faulty service-waiter to pieces—if she had worked there long.

She said she hadn't, but Martha had. And just then Martha came out the back, and I told them I had a class project for my next semester, and could anyone tell me anything unusual about the Subway.

Martha gave me this long, long look.

She was old, probably fifty, but okay. She tapped the fountain, and it gave her an apple cola, and then she leaned on the counter and looked into the middle of nowhere. "Y'know, kid," she told the nowhere she was looking at, "there ain't nothing *usual* about the Subway. Nothing at all. I tell you, I'm so glad to get outta here nights, you can hear me singing all along the pipe when I'm going home."

"It's true," said the other waitress.

"For starters," said Martha, "I used to work on Forever Avenue, up top. Had a room in a run-down boarding house. I always wanted to act. Never made it—Oh, nearly, once. Plenty of us like that. You don't wanna act, do you?" She shot me a searing glare. Her eyes were a weird kind of blue. I shook my head. "Well, anyway. Years ago I get the chance of a job down here with a lot more money, because all the mechanical systems are going wrong, all the robs are breaking down, and soon as they're fixed they quit again. So here I was, and it don't take me long to see something very unusual is going on. I mean, you ones that just come down then go up again, you miss a lot. What have you heard," she added, "so far?"

"Just what you said. Machines go wrong. And there's a phantom train—"

"Oh, that." Martha shrugged. "That train. Guess we've all seen some funny kinda train sometime. But maybe we were drunk. And maybe all the electrics and tech stuff causes all the failures, like they say. Or not," she added slyly. "But I tell you what gets to me. It's the *other* things."

"What things?"

"Sounds," said Martha. "*Smells. Creatures . . .*"

"Seeing things," cut in the other woman suddenly.

"Yeah sure, Olive-Alice. You've seen a few, am I right? And so have I. Most of us have, down here. And I tell you, they are some *strange* sights."

"Wh-what are they?"

But at this point Otis interrupted.

He put his paws up on the counter and peered watch-fully at Martha and Olive-Alice, with the sharper light he can switch on in his eyes.

Martha snapped, "That mutt real or robo?"

"He's—he's an S.C. Deluxe."

"Still don't know where those big gray feet've been."

Offended, Otis lowered his paws.

But Martha had lost interest in talking to me. She took her cola back to the kitchen.

I could have strangled Otis.

I stared at Olive-Alice. "What did you *see*?"

"Well, y'know," said Olive-Alice, "they say—I mean the management—better not talk about it. They say it's a kind of nondangerous sort of stuffy air thing down here sometimes, makes you think you see things aren't there. Only it's not dangerous. You just . . . see things."

"And hear and smell things," I prompted.

"It's just some music you hear. Could be from any-place. From up top, some movie orchestra."

"But all the stages are soundproof."

"Ah," said Olive-Alice, knowingly, "*so* they *say*."

OTIS'S DISKRIPT

"Why did you *do* that?" Jet demanded angrily the moment we were a few paces along the sidewalk.

I explained carefully.

"Neither woman was to be trusted. Especially not the Martha woman."

Jet paused. "Okay. You mean they were lying?"

"Not exactly. More exaggerating, perhaps."

"What does *that* mean?"

"Martha is a failed actress. But she has trained to *be* an actress. She overdramatizes. And with Martha, too, her whole *personality* struck me as *acted*."

"So it wasn't true."

"I can't tell if it was or was not. I'm not equipped with a lie-detection unit."

"Oh, Otis!" shouted Jet.

People on the sidewalk turned and smiled indulgently at a girl shouting at her very-likely-robot dog.

Jet hated this.

I was very sorry.

But a dog must do what a dog must do. Even an S.C. Deluxe.

ROOF-TOP PARTY: FREEZE FRAME

There is a scene. Only this is not a scene in a movie. This is a Scene with a capital *S*.

Among the night-lit lilacs and rose arbors atop the Fame Palace, Turquoise Latter, minor supporting actress in the now-filming top-budget cinematic experience *Fall of Super Troy* has just slung a full glass of red grape juice (containing also a spoonful of Rise-and-Shine—the product that makes Life go with a Wow) at her sister, Amber Latter.

Rector Pandion (worlds-acclaimed director of *Building Rome in a Day*, et cetera) stands scowling.

Sought-after actor Bronze Shunk (star of *Building Rome* and *Ben Hur 6*) and his latest female companion, Crimson Jones (star of *Ben Hur 6* and *Spartica*) stand laughing.

Jet's Journal

Otis and I had gotten to the swan fairly early. I had room service bring me a Kongburger—not bad. Then I went to bed and to sleep about ten P.M.

I am woken, and Otis is make-believe woken, about midnight.

We sit on the bed, ears up, listening.

Dad: "He may be famous on seven planets, he may be rolling in stollars, but he is old enough, Amber, to be your father. No—the guy is *older* than your damn father."

Mom: "Don't swear, honey."

Dad: "Damn swearing. Screw swearing."

Dad is *very* loud. "I'm ashamed of you, Amber. And to think, I sat and *drank* with him."

"*I'm* ashamed, too!" This shriek is Turquoise's. Unmistakable.

"Can it!" Dad. "I am sick to my stomach with the damn pair of you."

Turquoise weeps. No, she cries like a little kid.

Like I remember her crying years ago when she was only thirteen and I was only nine, and I crept out of bed and went to her bed and climbed in and put my arms around her, and then we both sobbed and I said, Turquoise, what's wrong? And she said, I failed my exam. I loved her, and I said she was so wonderful that it wouldn't count if she failed all her exams because in the end she would be a great movie star.

And now I could hear Amber start to cry, too, and then Dad slammed a door—it had to be him, Mom never does that—and then Mom murmured.

And I cried a bit, too. And I hugged Otis, and he licked my face. He smells of fresh salad. Not like a real meat-eating, nonflossing dog.

I'd figured out what must have happened. The man they'd been talking about wasn't Bronze Shunk, who isn't really old, only twenty-two. So it had to be someone else—and who else here had Dad taken a drink with but Reck Pandion?

I could sort of picture it. Turquoise trying to lure Bronze away from whatever woman had him, and Amber meanwhile somehow (*how?*) catching the eye of foulest old Wreck.

(And then I remember *Amber* when she was almost sixteen and I was almost fourteen, and she stood by the big full-length mirror, also crying, and saying over and over, Why am I fat? Why am I ugly? And she wasn't either, but I slunk away because even then I couldn't really talk to her anymore, and so anything I said wouldn't matter.)

I lie in the bed holding Otis so tight any real dog would whimper or bite or run, but Otis can handle it. I fall asleep with my head on Otis's tuft-fur flank. He has a mechanism he can activate to make it seem like he breathes. He does this for me, and it's the breathing rhythm that helps me sleep again.

Love you, Otis.

Love you—all. I wish—

I wish we were home. I wish none of this crap had ever happened.

3

![striped bar decoration]

Jet's Journal *(continued via Otis's Diskript)*

I walked out of the hotel about six the next morning, with Otis by my side. Today is Hereday, second day of the weekend, and tomorrow is Holiday, third and last day of the weekend. And I don't want to go back, not even when we get to Oneday. Or Twoday, or the whole rest of the week, or the year, however long we're stuck in this place.

As I went out the swan's front lobby I thought, I shouldn't do this. They'll worry.

But I wonder if they'll even notice.

Anyway, I left a note on the elecinstant pad: *See y'all later.*

The apartment had been silent, like no one but me was there. Not a sound. No tears or arguing, not even Dad snoring.

We went straight to the nearest pipe elevator and rode down to the Subway.

I bought a hot dog at a stand.

It didn't seem the same down here today.

There were already plenty of people around, and most of the stores and restaurants were open, and the trains ran, but somehow . . . I don't know.

It's a funny thing. Something about the light. I don't seem to cast a shadow here—I mean I just didn't see one anywhere for me or anyone else. And then suddenly, like when I turned off Welles onto Keaton, this huge enormous black shadow of me shot up to one side of me, all over this wall. And then it kind of wasn't there anymore.

I went in and out of stores, looked at books and camputers, jeans and lip gloss. I went to a movie theater and watched old movies and laughed a lot and then remembered about my family and stopped laughing.

By two in the afternoon, which I knew from all the electric clocks all over the Subway, which tinkle or beep or drum or clang, or even strike, each hour, sometimes with animated characters to act it out, too—I was depressed.

I mean, I was already. But now I had to think about it.

We sat on a bench and watched the trains.

"Otis, I guess we have to go back. They'll all be out someplace anyhow. That's if Wreckage didn't fire Turquoise and Turquoise didn't kill Amber. Or even if they did."

"There's Ben," said Otis.

I looked around, and there Ben was. He was standing under a fake tulip tree talking tensely into a call button on his sleeve.

"Hi, Ben," I said, when he'd finished.

"Uh—hi, Jet. Otis. How are you?"

"Okay. You?"

"Just lost another of my robs. Don't know where he went. He's a street-cleaner model. He was right behind me till we get to the closed pipe on Third Man Street. I mean right *there*. And I glanced around, and there he wasn't. I mean, I'd been checking his dust disc about two seconds ago."

"Could it have gotten in the pipe?"

Ben looked blank. Then he said in a flat kind of way,

36

"No. A closed pipe is *closed* in the Subway. They're the ones that run straight through from the studios up top and on down into the archives below us." Ben gazed around. He added, "I bet someone took him. But who'd be that quick?" Ben asked himself. "Milsner," he replied. Then he added, "I reported the loss, but maintenance won't come for another couple hours. If they ever do. I'll take myself off and look for that Milsner."

Little kids tag along with adults. You grow out of it, at least by eleven.

I tagged along with Ben as he went back up Third Man, went all around the closed pipe there—a smaller one, only about ten feet around and unpainted—and next on into a narrow street named only A7.

Otis paused to sniff the A7 sign, raising himself on his hind legs. When a real dog does something like that, the next thing he'll usually do is pee on the sign or the sidewalk or somebody's car. But, of course, Otis never needs to pee on anything.

"What is it, Otis?" I asked.

"A new smell. A live animal of some sort—something like a true canine, but also something else—a horse?"

37

Otis pondered. He sniffed again. Ben was walking on. "A *snake*," concluded Otis.

"Doesn't seem likely." I hadn't smelled anything like dogs or horses. I'd certainly never known what a snake smelled like. I mean, do they *have* a smell?

Ben had stopped. Then he looked back. "Uh, Jet. Maybe—I just thought. Let's say *ciao* here. This Milsner guy is a *type*."

I thought, Oh, he wants to get rid of me. Fine.

I said, "Sure."

But Otis surprised me, and maybe Ben, very much.

By shooting past us and running down Street A7, and turning the next corner at a rate of ten million miles per second, his tufty fur streaming in the whirlwind of his speed. He was gone.

"Oh, *OTIS*—" I screamed like some truly hopeless case, and pounded after him, and Ben charged after us both, around the corner of A7 and into another even narrower street, this one almost an alley.

The light was lousy here. No pretty parasol lamps, just some little dull globes high up at intervals, and most of these had gone out. I got the sense of lots of blank walls going by, the blind backs of warehouses. There was a flight of steps to one side, but so dark there you could hardly see it—and there was something else. Something else, just moving away across the dark, dark end of the dark street. A sort of shiny bluish shadow, moving, filmy, *glittering*—like a fish does through deep muddy water—

Otis had flattened himself down on his stomach on the ground, like a real dog.

I'd stopped dead. Ben, too, right behind me.

The three of us watched in total silence.

Last impression I had—yards and yards of thick, thick, glittery rope, so thick it was thicker than any rope could be, uncoiling, looping, *slithering* away.

"It's gone," I whispered.

Overhead one of the dead globes popped and flickered back to life.

Otis got up. His coat stood on end, just like the hair felt on my head.

"Ben, *what was that?*"

"Whoa." said Ben. "Just another of them."

"Another . . . of *what?*"

"Down here, off the main concourses. Now and then."

Now and then . . . *what?*" Never before had I managed to shout in a whisper.

"You see strange things. Hallucinations, they tell you. Stale oxygen."

Yeah. One piece of that was right. It had been a strange *thing.*

He went on, "It doesn't have to mean anything. Unless you let it."

"We both saw it. Otis *saw* it. Otis, you saw it, didn't you? You *chased* it."

Otis said, "I should *not* have chased it. That was very unnecessary of me. I have no DNA nor any natural instinct. Ridiculous."

I said, "Was it what . . . I thought?"

Otis replied in his most sensible tone, "It was a dragon."

AROUND THE CAMPFIRE: CLOSE-UP

Where the streets start to become alleys and stop having names (A1 to A9, B1 to B21, and so on), there are places where people *live—exist*, if you call it that, down here in Ollywood's Subway.

It happens everywhere, of course.

Some always fall through the net, of employment or stollars or family life, of self-worth, or just plain hope.

Though people have actually completely disappeared from the Subway under Studiocity, some also just become too hard to find. But then, no one wants to find them.

Ben wanted to find Milsner, however.

It took about two hours.

By then the clocks of the Subway were calling five P.M. earthclocktime.

Jet and Otis were still with Ben.

After they'd all seen the dragon, a kind of companionship had seemed to knit the three of them together.

Jet wondered if Ben didn't want to be alone. For herself she felt a combination of scared crazy—and madly curious. And Otis? Perhaps for a robot dog, the most interesting thing in his whole life had just happened.

And so then they came out of a tangle of extra-narrow alleys—in some of which Ben had to walk sideways to squeeze through—and there was broken paving and a ruined old bridge with the remains of rail tracks on top of it. One dead train balanced up there. It wasn't even a cute train, but painted gray. All the unbreakable windows in it were broken.

Under the bridge sat a group of filthy men dressed in bad clothing. And it was cold there, and they had lit a fire. But it wasn't a real fire. It was a big heating box, and a rusty glow flickered-flickered from its panel. Although this was not meant to happen, and might indicate the appliance was dangerous, it gave the odd effect of historic firelight. A soldier's campfire, perhaps, in a movie about Alexander the Great or the Pharaohs.

Ben did not speak to all the men in front of the fire. He let them all look up and growl, and then he spoke to the one man who didn't do either.

"Milsner."

"Yeah, Ben."

"You take one of my robs?"

"Tell me which. I'll tell you if."

"Dusty."

Milsner raised his battered, dirty face. He had been a handsome guy once. He had been in the movies once. But that was all of seven and three-quarter years ago.

"What I'd want with a dusting machine, Benny? Do I look like I dust a lot here?"

Jet's Journal (*cont.* VOD)

I sat quiet.

You bet I did.

When they passed around a filthy plastene box of some awful drink stuff, I was worried I'd insult them if I said no. But it was okay because Ben said for me, "She don't drink yet, guys. Don't turn her off a nice glass of wine when she's older." And the one Ben called Milsner grinned and said, "Right, Benny. This really *would* turn her off."

I don't know what was in it. It stank like the old gasoline no one uses now, except in specialty licensed cars.

Otis sat by me, bolt upright, watching, with the bright light on in his eyes.

(I just knew he was still blaming himself for reacting like a real dog to the dragon. Only thing is, wouldn't a real dog have just bolted the other way in terror?)

"That thing for real?" one of the hoboes (old word—but what they were, sort of) said to me, meaning Otis.

I wasn't sure what to say, but Ben said, "Yeah. It's real."

"Nice pooch," said someone else.

Otis allowed a couple who wanted to stroke him and scratch behind his ears to do so. He'd switched on his breathing, too, to look genuine.

After they'd had big drinks from the awful box—Ben took only a sip—a silence fell.

In the silence . . . odd sounds.

Drip-drip of water from someplace. Rustly noise, perhaps a rodent that had a home down there too. And then, far off, so faint I thought maybe I only imagined it, a drift of music, all sweet and slow. It wasn't like what the diners play. And anyhow, you don't hear any music from them once you're out the door.

Ben spoke from nowhere into the sort of haze that had settled: "Saw a dragon. Back of A7."

Some of the men murmured.

Only Milsner this time looked up. "Yeah, Ben? What kind?" (He had really good teeth, except one side tooth had broken off and never been fixed. I guess no dentist works that side of town.)

"Bluey outfit. Long tail. Wings folded. Head like a big dog."

"Yeah," said Milsner. Then, to my alarm, he looked full at me. "Little girl," said Milsner, "you saw it, too?"

"Yes."

"And was it a dragon?"

"I . . . think so."

"Better believe it. Listen," he said, and looked away up into the black roof of the bridge, "I was once on the shining dream-screen. I was once an actor. They called me Aragon O'Shane. Milsner's my real name—not strong enough, they said, so I had to be Aragon O'Shane. What do you think of that?"

"It's a good name," I said politely.

Still looking up into the bridge, he smiled.

He said, "I once starred in a pilot—know what a pilot is?"

"A movie they make to see if the idea will work, if people like it."

"You got it. They make the pilot, and then if it's a success with the great wise money people who run the show in Ollywood, they put it on the telecine. Then if that works, too, they make a series and everyone gets rich. Or they remake the movie for a bigger screen, and then maybe several movies—sequels, prequels. And everyone gets stinking rich. The pilot I starred in was called *Diamond City*. They said, *Aragon, we are going to make you an immortal.* Only the movie bombed. And instead of making me immortal, it made me Milsner again, and now I live here under a broken overpass."

I felt kind of sorry for him.

In fact, I felt *really* sorry for him.

Perhaps, before, I'd never felt so sorry for anyone who scared me like he did. I mean, the dragon didn't scare me like he did. I mean, it was a dragon, to be scared of it was natural. Milsner was human.

Ben said, "*Diamond City* was a great film."

"Sure," said Milsner.

And they passed around the box again.

But I could hear the music again, rising and falling. I could hear piano, or synthiano, and violins or viosynths. And then I fell asleep, sitting upright, leaning on Otis. Hey, Jet, bad move.

In my sleep I still heard them talking, only I was dreaming, too, their voices came through into the dream.

In the dream I was running, fast, and Otis was running fast beside me. Lots of levels went by, and huge round lens lights like the ones of overcameras, and railroad tracks and blank walls.

All the time I heard the hobo men talking.

"'Member *my* pilot, Mil?"

"*Into the Depths*. Another Atlantis, a lost city under the ocean . . ."

"'Member that sequence where I was riding the great fish, and I could breathe in the water?"

"Yeah, sure, sure. A great sequence."

"And what about *Gardens of Babylon*?"

"Yeah. Great."

Dreaming, I ran on and on.

But now and then, between the blank dream walls, I could see lengths of sparkling blue ocean with drowned Atlantis cities in them, or big fish swimming up the rail tracks with hoboes sitting on them, and over some of the higher Subway levels trailed pieces of the Hanging Gardens, with roses and monkeys in them.

But there'd been a long quiet now, no one saying a word, and then I heard Milsner say in his roughened velvety voice,

"Say, Ben, where'd this kid come from? She's dressed okay, and she has this smart modified dog, which if it isn't a rob then I'm Lassie. Her family are stollared-up rich, right?"

I couldn't hear Ben say anything.

"Strikes me, man," said Milsner, "if we hung on to her awhile, then sent somebody a call, that somebody might cough up something for her. Money. Whatever they think she's worth. Or better yet, if she has some relative in the movies—and I guess she may, because she sure knows what a pilot is—maybe the relative can find some way of giving us all a second chance in a picture. Eh, Ben? Even just a walk-on. Get my teeth fixed, do some workouts—I'd be okay. We'd all be okay, wouldn't we, huh?"

I heard Ben after all. He sounded frightened. "She's nobody, Milsner. Not worth a cent. Her mom works in a robo-laundry."

"No, Ben, that's a lie. Always know when you're lying, Benny. So, what do you say? You want to join the gang?"

"Mils—"

"Come on, buddy. You musta had this in mind. Kidnap and ransom. Or why bring her along?"

I heard Ben say bitterly, "I forgot what you're really like."

In my dream I thought Ben was getting up and Milsner, too—and there was a big soft kind of *thunk* noise, and then Otis, running by me in the dream, is pulling at my sleeve, and I hear Milsner grunt and then he says, "No, you bastard—you forgot what this *place* is like. Can't you feel the power of it anymore? All just trapped and waiting to bust free, like the lava in a volcano. And one day it'll blow. Inn-Die-Gaaray!" Milsner shouts. I think that's what it is—Inn-Die-Gaaray—then they all yell.

In the dream there is a blue-green flash. My eyes open, and Otis has bitten through my sleeve. He's never bitten me before; even now he hasn't broken the skin. But he's hauling me to my feet, and I'm staggering, and I see Ben and Milsner are rolling on the ground, punching and kicking at each other, and the others are leaping around them, looking terrified or angry or pleased, or all three, and then the heating box goes flying and there's a horrible crackling noise and white sparks running all over . . .

But now Otis and I are really running.

I'm still half asleep and I'm running.

"Where . . . we . . . going?" I gasp to Otis, who seems to be leading the way.

"Back to the main streets," he tells me, not needing to breathe as I do.

So we run. But behind us I can hear some of them coming after us. They're running, too. I hope it isn't Milsner. He's the worst. I want to go back to check that Ben is okay, but I can't make myself do that and I don't think Otis will let me.

I have no idea which way we have to go.

We're running through different areas from the ones we came by, but Otis has a directional thing in his head— he'll get us there.

Only what about Ben—

Now they're shouting after us.

They're calling me the worst names, the kind I'm not supposed to know exist or anyone uses.

There are at least five of them running behind us. I can't hear Milsner's voice though. I can't hear Ben's voice either.

Up a flight of stack-steel steps, along a gantry, ware-houses towering. Big shadows. My big shadow jet black, and Otis's shadow like a huge black wolf.

What if . . . the dragon ended up *here*?

And then I see the way ahead is blocked, shut off completely, by one of the biggest descending closed pipes. It's painted black, no pictures. It must be about a hundred feet around—and—

And is it just my eyes, my pulses jumping because I'm running—only—

Only *it* seems to pulse, the pipe—it's pulsing like a gigantic black heart.

I'm about thirty feet away. Otis springs around and cannons into me, and we fall in a heap.

"No farther, Jet."

"But . . . *they're* . . . just behind . . . us."

And they are, the men from under the bridge. They're scrambling up the stairway onto this gantry, grinning, looking like they're frothing at the mouth—

But *this*—is in front of us.

"I can defend you," says Otis. "Seven are a lot, I admit. But my teeth are a great deal better than theirs."

And I think that they'll kill Otis. No, I know he can't "die" but it'll amount to the same thing.

Then the black pipe makes its own strange noise.

It's sort of like the sound a strong wind makes blowing through trees in the fall. Also it's sort of like a big cold breath. My hair blows around my face, and Otis's fur is blown, and the hobo-actor men over there, they stop dead.

When I look back at the pipe, I think I'm still asleep after all, and that is fantastic since it will mean none of this other crap happened/is happening. Why do I think this? Because now, there in the pipe that has no pictures, I can see the dark sparkle of a far-off blue ocean.

And then . . .

Then the breath that just breathed out instead breathes *in*—and *in*—and *i-n-n-n* . . .

Otis and I are off our feet, hurtling backward, sideways, headfirst, upside down—through the air—and miles off the hoboes have gotten small as really ugly little dolls and the gantry and walls and the Subway and everything are going, going.

Gone.

GANTRY: EXTRA SCENE

As Jet and Otis are swirled away into the pipe—looking like they are being sucked inside a giant vacuum cleaner—and *vanish*, two other whirling objects fly out past them, blown in the opposite direction.

Impossible to be sure what *these* two things are.

But *whatever* they are, they rush on over the gantry and slam right into—right *through*—the reeling group of men, knocking them flying.

This pair of unidentified objects then spins off into the tangle of alleyways.

And they, too, are gone.

PART TWO

4

It is dusk.

A low sun is sliding, in a scarf of soft purple cloud, under the rim of a navy blue sea.

All around, the lush green of forest becomes dark. Shadows fill and condense the trees. Now the sea is darkening, too. Little ruffles of pearly foam gleam and go out and gleam again on a long beach, pale in daylight but now tinted blue.

Something stirs somewhere, a soft rippling sound: *hurrrh, hrrrr.* Some animal? A night wind rising?

The last slice of muffled sun sinks.

Stars light up overhead like tiny windows.

Everything is still now.

As if it holds its breath and waits.

OTIS'S DISKRIPT

Not to reckon myself more responsible is perhaps an error on my part, but I have to say in fairness that missing the half-yearly service is not recommended, and, of course, I have missed it. Otherwise, some slight weakness in my mental reflex would have been spotted and put right.

For I should have wakened Jet and gotten her away from danger much more quickly.

Since we left the hotel in Studiocity, she speaks her journal into my own recording device. Obviously, I never listen to what she says.

Nor do I need to listen to see she is both brave and scared by what has happened.

We do not know where we are. It is unlike the Subway, and unlike all the other places in Ollywood where we have been.

Jet's Journal (*cont.* VOD)

It's Holiday, the last day of the weekend, and here I am . . . *where*?

I know it's morning because the sun, which sank last night into the dark blue sea, rose ten hours later—by Otis's time reckoning—over the forest behind us.

During the night something in the forest made a weird loud sort of purring noise. And in the night, too, things flew over on huge wings—too dark to see what they were. We saw some birds this morning, but they were normal bird size. I don't think the night-flying things were birds at all . . .

No moon rose last night, like it does on Obelisk, or apparently on Earth, or Earthtwo.

Smell of forest and flowers and wet soil and the sea, and something else—neither Otis nor I know what.

While I slept, Otis kept guard.

This morning, of course, I woke in time to see the sunrise.

Don't know what I feel.

Well, scared.

Only . . . hungry, too.

Should we go to the sea's edge and catch a fish? Only I don't know how, nor does Otis. Anyhow, it might be poisonous. Otis says that nothing here is like the rest of the planet. He can't explain, doesn't know how it's different, only that it is.

This is much later. I think there's time to put this onto the disc. If any of them look in, I'll stop.

They think I'm just talking to my dog.

They don't think my dog can understand, let alone talk, let *alone* record.

A lot has happened.

They just came out of the forest with the splintery sunlight behind them. About eleven tall guys and women, tanned, good-looking, and young. Long shining hair down their backs. They wore tunics and boots and stuff like that, and they carried spears and things, and they looked—well, they *were*—like they were from about twenty-five centuries and a whole lot of planets ago. Like people were on Earth, back when the ancient Greeks and Romans were around.

I just sat there on the beach with Otis.

And these people stopped and stared at *us*.

In a while they spoke to each other in a foreign language I didn't understand.

Then one of the men spoke directly to me.

"Ardla evik con blay." At least it's what I thought he said.

I stared. Then shook my head.

The guy craned forward and repeated the words very slowly and loudly. *"ARDLAAA EVIKK CON BLAYY."*

"Sorry, I don—"

And something even crazier happened.

A jumble of palish lights skidded across the scene in front of me, low down, about knee-high. And they looked like—well—like *words* in *English*. It could have been a trick of the light, except Otis whispered, *"Subtitles!"* And then Otis read off from memory—the words had already gone out—what apparently the man had said to me with all that *ardlaaa* stuff. Which was: *Are you a sea woman?*

So I just said, "No, I'm a stranger here."

And then something else sort of happened in the air, only I couldn't figure out what, and the man *said* in

English, "You are from the Outer Land. An Arriver."

"Er . . . yeah."

Then all the warrior-looking people on the beach murmured, and I understood every word, which was pretty much what he and I had just said. But it, too, was all in English.

Then one of the women strode forward. She had long blond hair, nearly as good as Turquoise's. "You will come with us."

An offer I'd better not refuse?

"Okay. Whatever."

She lowered the spear she'd been pointing at me.

I thought how attractive they all were, and how *clean*. They even smelled nice—with a hint of expensive cologne. Basically, apart from their clothes, they looked and smelled pretty much like well-off, well-groomed people usually do.

And that did *not* tie in with the look of their clothes and weapons—except the clothes looked laundered, even the random hole or tear, even the *stains* looked laundered. And their weapons were all polished and shone like their well-shampooed and conditioned hair.

"You will go with us now back into the forests," said the man who spoke to me first. "Be aware, the trees are full of dangers. We risked them to fish here. You have cost us the catch. Now you must keep quiet and obey. If you attempt any disruptive act, we shall slay you on the spot."

Yay.

"Sure," I said. Of course.

"Your hound may come with you," Blondie added. "He is a fine brute."

In some ways the forest was like the forests at summer camp, when I was a kid.

Huge soaring black-wood pines and arbor oaks and what looked like Earth-import beech trees. But there were other trees I'd never seen on Obelisk, or even on a screen or in a book. There were things like purplish-green broccoli, and there was a very short tree that was nearly blue and had big roselike flowers. And sometimes flying bugs flew into the roses and the roses snapped shut and I thought, Yuck, it's like a Venus flytrap. Only after a second the rose opened and out flapped the bug, all happy, and zizzled off. (*Zizzle* was the sound their big lilac or red wings made.) Occasionally, one of the zizzlers landed on one of the warrior band. To be honest, I hoped none of them would get in my hair.

My captors guided me away from some long spiky ferns. These ferns, Blondie told me, lash out and sting. When you looked, you saw little bits of bone around their roots—I assumed things they'd caught for lunch. Luckily I didn't see anything like that happen.

Sometimes lean rodenty critters scuttled by. They had moss growing in their fur. Otis told me it was camouflage, but one of the warriors hissed I must stop my hound from making noise.

In fact, they all moved silently as the sunlight. Even Blondie, when she told me about the ferns, spoke very low in my ear.

Once an awful animal slunk across the clearing ahead. It was like nothing I saw even in my worst dreams ever: blotchy dark and hairless, with a kind of long, pleated nose. It looked right at us with pale gray eyes, and all the band leveled their spears at it or raised their bows and arrows. But it only blinked and slinked on into the black-wood pines.

I'd forgotten I was hungry because now I was so thirsty.

Finally Blondie looked around, then softly told one of the others, "Give the Arriver girris."

So the man thrust this leather bottle at me.

I glanced at Otis.

He leaned in and whispered, "I think it's all right. My analysis unit—"

"You said everything here was different and might be poisonous!" I irritatedly whispered back.

The man pushed the bottle right into my face and said, "*Take. Drink.* Cease *talking*. There is danger *everywhere*."

The girris stuff smelled wonderful—blueberries and ice cream. It tasted even better. I stood and thought, Am I in big trouble now? But I felt a lot better, so I drank some more.

When I tried to hand the bottle back, the warrior waved it and me away. It wasn't him being generous. I could tell he didn't want it near him now I'd used it.

Then we came to the top of a rise, and below the forest fell away for thousands of miles, it looked like, under a wide blue sky.

All of them stopped.

Blondie said, "Now we cannot avoid entering a place of Them."

Them definitely had a capital *T*. "Who?" I said.

She gave me a look.

"If you make any noise here, we must kill you instantly. Be aware, even with the softest tread, still we may all die."

I wished I hadn't had the girris.

Them.

Oh yes.

Them!

Before we'd gotten very far I noticed a new kind of tree.

They were *really* weird.

For a start, nothing else grew around them. The earth was churned up, big stones and roots lying everywhere, and once or twice big bare hills of earth rose higher than the trees. It looked as if something must have burst up from inside the ground.

As for the new trees, they were enormous. They had

66

no leaves. The bare bark was gray and shiny and seamed, and all of them were folded over and twisted around themselves. Sometimes moss or vines grew on them. And just sometimes they had, each of them, one or two small shiny slots high up, and these were a kind of shiny *sulky* green.

Otis seemed tense, but he didn't make a sound. And I didn't dare ask.

As for the warrior band, they *crept* along.

I began to be very, very frightened, and I didn't know what of.

In stories it's always the *new* one, the stupid youthful hero, who makes a mistake. I was pleased this *wasn't* my fault.

Though they had such great skills for moving silently, one of the guys up front stumbled and stepped on a piece of twig, and it snapped.

The sound ripped through the air, and everyone froze; just up ahead, fewer than fifteen feet away, one of the bare folded trees *came alive*.

It happened in fast slow motion.

I saw a body like a huge python uncoiling, and great

bat wings drawing back, and a head like a snake's head but with sticking-up ears. Two eyes, slots of sulky green, opened wide, and then its jaws opened much, much wider.

It made a noise like you do before you sneeze, and then it either sneezed or snorted out a vast whoosh of black-white-brown rushing, noisy snot-lava.

Everybody fell flat. Otis was on top of my head, and I couldn't see or breathe.

Rocks and stones rattled all around. Some hit me, small ones and not badly, glancing off, and there was the strong smell of wet clay and fresh-dug earth.

Then somebody—it was the blond woman—was pulling me up. And she yelled *"Run!"*

And we were all running, no longer trying to be quiet, through a dark mist of falling earth particles and pebbles, flying leaves and squashed berries, and someone was dragging me and I couldn't see.

And then we were out into broad daylight again, with ordinary trees widely spaced all around us. But the thing, which had been a *dragon*, only not like the one I'd seen on A7, or ever heard of, was far behind. When I looked

68

back, through the mist I could see that part of the forest we had just escaped was now a large hill of bare
crumbled earth and boulders, with the broken limbs of
trees sticking out.

One minute passed. Then Blondie spoke up, as if nothing special had happened. "On now." And to me, "The
huttra is just beyond that rise."

5

THE HUTTRA: PAN

View of a long plateau beyond the forest, with a few of the larger forest trees dotted over it, and now fruit trees and vines.

Some abnormally large flying creatures are wheeling high overhead on spiky wings. (Wingspan approximately twenty-five feet). They seem to have beaked heads, and *tails*.

The plateau lies on a cliff with the sea beyond and below. Faint cloud froths the horizon.

The huttra—hut village—is made up of stone huts.

They vary in size, and some are set in groves of fruit trees. Outdoor fire pits smoke. Here and there are metal baskets on poles, which hold fire at night.

The usual ancient activities go on: vine tending, bread making, weapon maintenance. There are no vehicles, nothing resembling a horse. There *are* dogs, lean and long-legged. Children rush about.

The huttra appears well established. It's been there since before any of its present people can remember.

Roughly in the center is a huge open well, or cistern, where people gather water and linger to gossip.

Across the open place with the well stands the largest hut house. It has patterns painted on the walls, and the doorway has two squat stone pillars. Outside, from the pole of a fire basket, hangs a kind of banner in red and yellow.

Everyone in the huttra turns to stare as the warrior band returns with Jet and Otis.

Jet's Journal (*cont.* VOD)
I couldn't figure out why the people in the huttra village didn't go down the cliff to the ocean, and fish.

As we walked through everyone *stared*. I went red and pretended I hadn't.

Then a lot of big dogs came bounding over to Otis.

I was so proud of him because he acted just like a real dog; you know the way they act. And the thing is the really real dogs don't behave like that to Otis, they *know* inside of about two seconds that he is *not* the same as they are. But here the dogs—the *hounds*, as these people call them—acted like Otis was *just* the same.

When he wouldn't leave me, they backed off, but several kept coming up, wagging their tails, sniffing, and nose-butting Otis.

There was a round walled pool, and on the far side a bigger hut. And the blond woman said, "There is the High House."

The hut isn't high, just a bit bigger.

But suddenly out strode this guy. It was Milsner.

Yeah. Milsner. Who wanted to kidnap us under the bridge in the Subway.

Only thing was . . . though I could clearly see it *was* him, it *wasn't*. Or, not like I'd seen him last.

This Milsner was strong and lean and tanned and fit, and he was truly handsome. I mean, Bronze Shunk was nothing compared to how Milsner looked now. Even I could see it. Milsner was about six four, and he had dark gold hair that hung down his back like it does with the others here. And his great dark eyes were—*beautiful*. And his teeth were perfect.

He spoke instantly to the band, and for a moment all I could hear again was that language they spouted when we first met them. *"Char garamaj?"* he said. *"Harn con bunder?"*

Then the subtitles flapped along the ground, and I read them.

He'd said: "Is *this* good fishing? Are they from hell?"

Charming.

But the band guy said angrily, "No, Aragon. You know not. They are out-things, Arrivers."

Hey, we were out-things now.

But Milsner spoke again, and it was in English.

"Yes, you have it right." And then he stared at me, and I could see, I *knew*, *this* Milsner hadn't ever laid eyes on us before.

OTIS'S DISKRIPT

My mental units are working overtime attempting to analyze all this. I believe I begin to understand. One thing stands out at once. The man who is a younger and more effective—not to mention *better*—version of Milsner is *not* Milsner at all. The name of Aragon, which the original Milsner said was given him, is apparently this man's true name.

The dogs are interesting in another yet similar way. They are not exactly dogs. Just as all the humans here are not exactly human, and Milsner—here—is not exactly human either. And yet they are all alive.

All of them seem too incredibly healthy and fresh— that is, hygienic. Which one would not expect of a primitive society such as this appears to be, let alone a dog in such a situation. (In fact, the dogs don't smell like any dog I've ever met before, not even like a robot dog, frankly. And, meanwhile, I can tell from their behavior and signals they think *I* am real in every doggish way.)

Jet bears up well. She is speaking her journal to me at this moment. Of course, as I explained, I never listen in, and so am free to be "writing up" my own.

Jet's Journal (cont. VOD)

Milsner, who is Aragon here, spoke to me.

"Perhaps you will be of use to me. Since you are from the other world, as *she* is."

What intense eyes.

I scowled at him because his look right then was too much. "I'm *not* from the sea."

"No, I think you are not. But *she* is, and she, too, does not belong in my world. You, in any case, do not resemble the people of Diamond City."

That clicked. *Diamond City* was the title of the pilot the first Milsner had starred in.

Aragon-Milsner turned on his heel—don't see that often—and strode back in his High House.

One of the other men then told me I had to go and wait in some other hut, but as he marched us along there he told me, "Diamond City lies beneath the waves."

Couldn't think of a reply to that. But when we reached the hut, I asked, "Am I a prisoner?"

"Perhaps," said the warrior. "Until we know you better."

"And then?"

"Then," he said with a nasty grin, "we may cast you back into the forest, for the earth dragons."

I don't know whose hut this was, but they've left it all to me for now. People keep coming to the door and looking in. Mostly they just seem curious. They like Otis and bring him food he politely, and nonspeakingly, refuses. A woman brought me fruit. It looks furry like peaches, but is orange and tastes like apples. Confusing.

The day seemed unusually short. I didn't imagine this—the previous night took around ten hours, Otis said, so the day should have lasted about fourteen, because Obelisk is like Earth, with a twenty-four-hour clock. But this day was six hours. Suddenly the shadows were long and the sky was pinkish purple, and when I stuck my head out of the hut, the sun had already vanished behind the forest. The other way along the plateau the sea was melting into the darkening sky.

The people here lit torches and the things up on poles, and in the other huts' window places were flickery candles that smelled like scented stuff you buy for presents. The woman came back with one of these for me, and a dish

of meat—but *what* meat? When I asked, she said, *Slurga.*
With no subtitles.

I didn't eat much, and only after Otis said it was harmless and probably some kind of deer. It was okay-ish.

I fell asleep after that. Not for long, but I had a really strange dream, but since everything is now so crazy, why worry about a *dream* being strange? But I dreamed I was back in Studiocity, in the hotel apartment in the swan.

I was up in the ceiling looking down, the way it sometimes is in a dream. The problem with this was, I could see *myself*. I was sitting on a couch in the main room, and Otis was down there, too, and I was laughing and he was barking, which he hardly ever does. Mom and Dad and Amber were standing across the room and shouting at us in absolute *horror*. Not that there's anything so new in Amber doing that. One other detail: the windows were completely smothered in weed-guano. You couldn't see out.

What woke me was a lot of calling and shouting outside the hut.

I knew at once where I was, and I thought one of the earth dragons had left the woods and come to attack us.

But when I'd run out on the track, I saw everybody was up on the headland, where the plateau stops above the sea. They were standing there in the dark looking out, illuminated by the fires in the village.

Only there was a glow, too, shining up out of the darkness where the sea was.

So I went to look, too, and where some women were standing I gently elbowed my way through. And the glow shone out there on the water, and it came from a great golden ship.

I suppose you expect to see a ship on the sea. And here, an ancient sort of ship, which this was. It had a great swooped-up front and a swooping-up back, too, both like the tails of huge golden fish. And there were three long, high triangular sails, but they were silver. Like the stuff they make expensive gowns from.

And there were oars. It was a *galley*, I remembered; the old ships that had to be rowed—they were called galleys. The oars were covered in silver and gold. And the whole ship was lit by this fierce yet pearly light, soft *and* brilliant at the same time.

There were lights floating in the water, too, but also very

big creatures swimming alongside the ship. Parts of their backs came up and then went down. I thought maybe they were whales—but they looked blue or green, and their skins were metal-glittery, more like fish.

A soft watery music was playing . . . from nowhere. It had harp sounds and little tinkly bells. But the decks looked empty.

While the ship sailed slowly by, all the people from the village gazed down at it. But then all their heads turned another way, to the right. I turned, too, and there was Aragon, whom I won't call Milsner anymore.

He stood just beyond the rest of us, and he fixedly stared out at the ocean. He looked angry. And astonishing.

In my ear one of the women was quietly saying something. "That is the vessel of their High Queen, Bekmira Ren. Aragon saw and met with her long ago, in battle. Now he can never forget her. But she is a sea demon, and he is a mortal man."

Beside me Otis cleared his throat. He'd told me that none of the people in the huttra *were* quite human. But the woman only thought Otis was growling. "The hounds always growl when the golden ship passes," she remarked.

"None of us go to fish from the beaches below, for the sea-demon city lies beneath this water."

"Oh, right." But I was curious. "Does Aragon always, er . . . react like this?"

"He has sworn to destroy the queen and her kingdom. Our gods demand it. The sea people are enemies to all who live on the land. And long ago *our* people ruled the Diamond City, and our own ships traveled everywhere, and we were rich and mighty. But then came a great wave, and our city sank beneath the ocean. And *she* came to rule there. Aragon, our prince, through his strength and will, shall one day win it back for us, and again glory will be ours."

The way she spoke, the way they all did—I should have worked it out much sooner. This was *dialogue*. And not that good . . .

Otis has said he already knew by this point. But I only figured it out right then, when the gold-silver ship glowed off around the sea beyond the edge of the cliff, the escort of sea dragons with it.

I said to the woman, trying to sound a bit more like they all do here, "Pray, what do you call this country?"

And she answered, "Indigara."

It was enough like the words Milsner and his gang had yelled in the Subway: *Inn-Die-Gaaray*. Enough like it to be the same.

PRODUCTION NOTE: OTIS'S DISKRIPT

The name *Indigara*, earlier pronounced *Inn-Die-Gaar-Ray*, quite obviously is formed from the first two letters of the titles of four movies, shot in Studiocity as the pilots for series which, in fact, along with many others, were never made. As follows:

Into the Depths. Diamond City. Gardens of Babylon. And (this fourth film I had really to search my memory banks for) *Race of the Dragons*.

So far as I can tell from my film index, *Into the Depths* was about a city lost in the sea, a sort of new Atlantis. *Diamond City* was about an ancient land city that had been invaded, its original people thrown out and forced to live as primitive hunter warriors. *Gardens of Babylon* was a fanciful retake on the mythical Hanging Gardens of ancient Babylon. *Race of the Dragons* was a fake semidocumentary about four types of invented dragon, representing the four elements of earth, air, fire, and water.

(Something strikes me here. Jet and I have seen in the forest the earth dragons, which breathe out earth. The sea dragons I think we saw with the gold ship, and no doubt they breathe out water. Air dragons, too, we've spotted, flying over. They must breathe out air. But fire dragons? Fire dragons that breathe out fire? This is rather concerning.)

Aside from that, I can only think this place we've been dragged into is a mixture of all four pilots. They have lain in Ollywood's archives and fermented like compost. They have come to life. And interbred. This is the result. Though S.C. Deluxe prepares us with thorough training, I hardly think I was ever prepared for something like this.

6

On the evening of Hereday, when the Latter family had finally calmed down after the roof garden picnic, Turquoise came over to the hotel, and Reck Pandion even turned up with a case of iced champagne.

Turquoise apologized to Amber and Amber to Turquoise. Reck put his arm about Amber. Amber burst into tears.

Dad became angry then calmed down because Mom kept murmuring that Reck was really a good guy, so talented, and he had seventeen houses on this planet alone and Amber might now have a chance in the movies, too.

83

Turquoise, who, over the weekend, had met a promising young actor called Bat Temperance (a minor prince in *FOST*), was much more forgiving, and took Amber's side.

Dad was outnumbered and outgunned. He shook hands with Reck.

After all this, they remembered they hadn't seen Jet for a while.

"She's still out at the park," suggested Amber.

"At twelve midnight?" gasped Mom. "No, she must be in her room here."

"Sulking," agreed Amber. But Reck glanced Amber's way, looking surprised, so she smoothly added, "No, poor kid. She's probably been upset by all this."

Turquoise went and flung open Jet's door—having shouted Jet's name first to warn her.

But Jet wasn't in there. Nor Otis.

A note was on the elecinstant pad: *See y'all later.*

It was exactly thirty-nine hours since Jet had last been seen by any of them, so far as they knew.

Reck said manfully, "Don't get upset, people."

He told them nobody could get lost here (having either

forgotten or never known or known but not believed the tales of persons vanishing from the Subway).

He called Security. Soon they could watch from the windows, between lots of little machines busily cleaning off weed-guano, Ollywood's famous private cops, the OPD, whirling along the avenues below, blue lights flashing.

By two A.M. various girls had been found in various parts of Studiocity—swimming in fountains, sitting in trees, spraying graffiti on the sides of movie lots, on statues of starlets from long ago. A couple of these girls were even brought to the apartment in the mistaken idea they were Jet. There they caused a lot of noise and ate the pan-crème chocolates Reck had also brought. One even bolted some champagne and then threw up on the rug.

At three A.M., all the non-Jets evicted, and the cleaning machine finally done with the rug, Reck departed for his penthouse suite on Screen Giants Boulevard, yawning at them as he went: "'S okay, folks. You'll have her back soon."

Which at five A.M. that very morning of Holiday, proved true. Apparently.

Everyone else by then was exhaustedly fast asleep.

But Jet and Otis, it seemed, were full of energy, and also hungry.

Laughing and barking (and, in fact, sometimes Jet also barked), they turned on all the maintenance machines in the outer room. Dusters, vacuum cleaners, window wipers, fans, heat system, air-conditioning, music center, telecine (even the rug cleaner came out and started again on the now totally cleansed rug), plus the food maker and toaster and juice creator and Coffee-often at the breakfast bar.

To those asleep, this sounded like an invasion from another planet.

Bleary-eyed and panic-stricken, the four other Latters erupted from their rooms, Turquoise—who had slept over—dashing in first.

Turquoise and Amber were the first to scream, too.

"What in the—?" cried Dad.

"*Jet*—what are you *doing*?" screamed Mom, who never did scream, so her scream was not as good as Turquoise's or Amber's.

"She's gone nuts!" shrieked Turquoise.

"She's horrible!" shrieked Amber.

But Jet and Otis, covered in raspberry jam and orange

juice, sprang on a couch and sat there, laughing and barking. Mini dust-imps whizzed through the air, and a succession of untended pancakes took off from the bar to land *kersplat* on the ceiling.

Jet's Journal (*cont.* VOD)

He called me up to the High House soon after sunrise the next morning. It hadn't been much of a night either, about three hours, Otis said. Felt like three minutes.

Inside the house was hung with painted cloth. He was sitting on a wooden bench with a sword across his knees.

Not a bad sword, though. Nice and bright and everything, with some notches worn along the sides of the blade, which must mean he's used it a lot.

We stood there, and he looked gloomily at us.

He spoke.

"I never saw a hound the likes of that one." Then he surprised me. "They say your name is Jet, like the black gemstone."

In the real world, people often think I was named for some kind of old flying craft. They ask if my second name is *Plane*.

But they don't have aircraft here, even old ones. Only golden silver galleons, and winged dragons which maybe *do* fly. (Were those big birds I saw in the sky on the way in here really dragons?)

I nodded.

"Tell me," he said, "about the world you come from."

I thought of how he was Milsner, there.

"I'd rather know about *this* one."

"Perhaps we can exchange our knowledge. Sit," he added, all lordly, but he is a lord here, so I sat on the other bench. Then a woman appeared with breakfast— wonderful-smelling new-baked bread, nuts and fruit.

He didn't really tell me anything about Here. And frankly I didn't say anything about where I came from.

I kept *wanting* to say, But don't you know none of this is for real? And *you're* not real? You're a character out of a movie pilot who's come to life in the shape of the actor who once acted it/you, and is now a bum who wants to kidnap people. And everyone else is the same, I guess, which is why you are all so clean and smell of af- tershave and perfume. And the hounds are like that, too. And as for the trees and landscape and the sea, and the wildlife and *especially* the dragons . . . They're probably just supremistic high-tech imaging that's also—come to life.

But I *didn't* say this.

It seemed really rude, for one thing.

And he'd never believe it. He thought he was real. They all must. Like if someone came up to me out of nowhere and said, Hey, Jet, someone just invented you and then you came to life, I would say, Go and jump up your own butt.

Besides, even though I *know* Otis is right about all this, Indigara is totally convincing when you're in the middle of it.

Or is it just I've never been all that at home in my own world, so I like it here because I'm *used* to not feeling *at home*?

And anyhow, Indigara is beautiful—thrilling, challeng-ing—even I can see that.

And it's clear that Aragon is *obsessed* with this Sea Queen Bekmira Ren. And I don't just mean because her people stole his city.

He just started talking about her. Like that other

woman said, he met the queen in battle, he got rescued from his sinking ship or something, and then was caught by her fleet, only later he escaped (and it does sound just like one episode in a series, doesn't it?). But anyway, he and she spent some time together. It seems her hair is black as a "raven's wing," but her eyes are the color of "violets." Oh, and pardon me, I forgot, her skin is like "cream."

I get the picture. He *likes* her.

After we'd had our chat, or rather he'd talked my ears off going on about *her*, Aragon announced that tonight he and I would go down to the beach below the cliff, and "scan the ocean." He said his people still keep their ships there, in caves. One day they will use these ships against Diamond City. And then suddenly he waved me off, so I left the house. And even as I did, the sky started to change.

It was a little scary.

Otis and I stared up, but we were the only ones. Naturally, everybody else took no notice. They're *used* to it.

You could see the sun actually *move*. It went sparkling over above, now and then in swirls of cloud that appeared and faded in seconds, and reached the tops of the forest to the west, and then glided right down among the branches. The sky smoothly changed from blue to smoky gold. And then to smokier pink.

"Wow, Otis, morning and afternoon all gone in—*how* long did it take?"

"Approximately one hundred and twenty seconds. Two minutes."

There've been times in my life I'd have *loved* time to go that fast. Like in math class, for example. Or when there's an argument at home. But then again, if life there was like here, when something dramatic happens, even if it's bad, time could slow right down instead. Two bad minutes could stretch to half an hour—or half a day!

Because everything runs on movie time here. When the scene is dramatic, it lasts, and when the script says: *Cut to*—

And it had cut to evening now.

And here came Aragon striding out, and here I was all ready (since I'd never had time to go anyplace else), and now we'd go down to the beach.

Three of the warriors went with us: a woman and two men.

The way down the cliff was pretty grim. And it was getting dark now, too.

A narrow slippery path came first, then a kind of natural stair. Some of the steps were crumbled and they all sloped, and some were shallow and some steep—about a foot deep each time. The woman warrior helped. In the end we just had to climb down the cliff face because the stairs stopped around twenty feet from the beach. (They'd been very surprised how well Otis managed—in fact, better than I could.) But they'd brought ropes and hooks with them so we could climb back up again.

By the time we were on the beach full night had come.

The sky was black velvet. Stars drizzled overhead.

Of course, no one lit a lamp.

I'd wondered what we were really doing. Looking for the golden galley to come back? Was it going to? Then what? And why did he want me here, too?

I soon found out.

Aragon took me aside, and we ambled off along the sand, with Otis padding quietly a few feet behind.

"Jet," said Aragon, "let me confide in you."

When older people say this kind of thing to me, I get kind of cautious. I said nothing.

Aragon spoke. "Here is the great secret, which perhaps already you know. *She*—their Sea Queen, Bekmira—is not of their kind. Nor of mine. But of *yours*."

I had this sudden feeling I really *was* in a movie, and I'd better come up with the right lines.

So I dramatically gasped, *"My* kind?" But I thought, What does he mean, *my kind*?

"She, like you, is one of the Arrivers. She comes from that other world that lies beyond this."

Screw the movie. "The Subway up top?" I heartlessly asked.

He took no notice of that.

"You and she truly are of the same people. People of a world that is not this one. Not Indigara. You see"—he has a great voice—"we met in battle, she and I. And though neither of us struck a blow against the other . . . a blade has pierced my heart."

I thought, Whoever wrote this dialogue needs some strong coffee. Or some ice water in his face.

I *said*, "You kind of love her, right?"

"No. *No.* Ah, Jet, wise child. Yes. I love her. Your youthful innocence sees through the walls of my heart. I shall no longer lie to you."

Child! It's typical.

We'd wandered off quite a way down the beach. The warriors had been left behind. I imagined they might be saying to one another resignedly, *Bet he's telling that girl all about how he loves the damn Sea Queen.* But perhaps they weren't—perhaps they were as dumb as he was.

The huttra cliff, and now other cliffs—these crowded by thick forest—leaned over us against the dark starry sky. Farther off were some huge cave openings; that was probably where they stored their ships.

Aragon paused. He looked up at the stars. "There may be some way that you could go to her, to Bekmira, claim kinship. Then . . . you could speak to her of me."

I was *not* keen on this idea. (Something like this had happened last semester. I'd been asked to tell a girl this guy liked her, and then had to come back and tell him she didn't like *him*. Gross. And both of them had gotten angry with *me*. What if this queen got angry with me? She was a *queen*!)

94

I was trying to think of a polite way to explain that, really, if he wanted someone to tell old Becky Ren he loved her, it should be him.

By then there was no good light anywhere, not enough stars and no moon. I looked at the black sheet of the sea and asked myself, how was I supposed to go to her anyway? I can swim, but she was down in the depths, wasn't she? Was he planning to drown me?

And then I dimly saw some kind of fish swimming at the dark edge of the beach, only it swam right in and stood up and waded out—and now it was running toward us and there was more than one—lots more than one—and I said "Er, Aragon—" But that was when the huge net descended over my head and over Otis as well, and ground and sky were reversed, and everything went fast. Then it was black-dark, and I was very wet, and I was in the ocean and . . . I don't remember.

OTIS'S DISKRIPT

Our attackers appeared to spring from nowhere. But I am fairly sure they were hiding in the caves below the cliffs. The other men ran out of the sea.

As the net came down, Aragon was already fighting, while his warriors were racing along the beach toward us. Swords flashed and there was shouting, and the sort of cursing one hears only in films for the whole family.

The people who had gotten hold of Jet and myself, however, were already dragging the net into the water. Even my teeth were unable to bite through the strands of the net. It seemed quite flimsy, but as this place is unreal, I suppose an *unbreakable* net might exist. The black water covered us.

Two points:

Point 1. It is normally impossible for humans and other land animals to breathe underwater without diving gear and oxygen. Nevertheless, I could see at once that not only the Sea People (who seem quite human but are actually only more characters from the movies) could breathe, but that Jet was breathing, too, exactly like she had out in the air. The seawater is faintly salty in smell, and is felt slightly against the skin, but in no other way, chemical or organic, is it at all like any sea, either on Earth or any of the habitable planets (such as Obelisk). I have been unable to analyze *what* this sea is made of.

Point 2. Jet was unconscious. This concerned me only for a moment, because the next second so was I. It's fairly obvious that a robot dog, let alone an S.C. Deluxe, simply can't *become* unconscious, unless it switches off its mechanism on purpose. I hadn't. Yet unconscious I was.

And so we were hauled through and down into the strange ocean of Indigara, and neither of us saw any of the journey.

When I came to, however, I found that my brain had worked out the real name of the Sea Queen Bekmira Ren, and therefore who she must really be.

Jet's Journal (*cont.* VOD)

When I woke up again, I was lying in this enormous room. I stared up and up at the ceiling about eighty feet over my head. It was polished marble like in a museum. Everything was lit by these tall gold lamp holder things, the shape of giant fish standing on their tails, with the glowing lamps clenched in their mouths. There were pillars. And some plants in big vases with perfumed flowers. The couch I was lying on felt like silk, and it was scattered with plum red pillows. Otis was lying on my feet and was staring around like I was.

But everything there was *nothing* compared to the other thing.

The room was full, wall to wall, floor to ceiling, with *water*.

You could see through it. Now and then, it gave a little ripple. And now and then, too, some schools of little fish would come swimming through, darting and playing, not seeming bothered about anything. Some even perched on the flowers in the vases. One came up and circled Otis's head. Otis snorted—never heard him do that before—and the fish took off.

I'd opened my mouth in a gasp of amazement, and when I let my breath out, I realized I'd inhaled the water into my lungs. *Then* I realized I must have been doing it the whole time. And it wasn't uncomfortable. I hadn't drowned.

I must have looked terrified. Otis put his paw on my knee. He said quietly, "This isn't real water. That is why it's breathable. It's a special effect."

"I.T. Supremistics. *Imaging*. But it feels real . . . "

I sat up and swung my legs off the couch. I felt fine, though something must have knocked me out (I hadn't *passed* out. I don't), and I was breathing water. I swooshed my hands about, and ripples wildly sped in all directions. But even weirder, my hair wasn't swirling about the way it would in ordinary water. Otis's coat lay flat and tidy. "Look at the lamps," I added to Otis. (Our voices sounded perfectly normal, too.) "They're burning, the flames in them are burning *in the sea*—and they flutter only a bit, as if there's just a slight breeze . . ."

There was sudden loud splashing, though, in a big open window across the room. The window showed a background of cascading seaweed, and an old woman who was rushing up through it, splashing.

She was a crazy old woman, too, with spiky, raggedy gray hair standing on end and a long dark epic-movie-type robe. She thrashed her arms and made faces at me. Then she screamed, *"Beware the dragon of fire!"* And vanished behind the weeds.

I might have discussed this with Otis, but the *next* second two big doors opened and a couple of girls sort of flew into the room.

They started laughing as soon as they saw me. But, oh my. They had the best hair and all wound through with pearls and shells, and elegant long dresses, and really great makeup, which hadn't washed off.

"Pm bss yn cooroo, sll Bekmira," said one.

I stood there waiting until the subtitles came up. She'd said, "You must come with us now to Bekmira's audience chamber."

So Otis and I, of course, went.

The shock was wearing off. In the wide corridor, with men in golden fish-scale armor standing to attention all along it, the two pearly girls started swimming. So Otis and I did, too.

When we reached the audience chamber, which was marble and gold like all the rest, and like the rest full of water and fish, I had my first view of Diamond City. This was because there was one huge window instead of a fourth wall.

You'd expect Bekmira's palace to be high up, and it was. From here you could see down and over everything. It was very impressive.

Great big buildings, big as anything in a modern real-world city—and you'd never have to climb stairs for a hundred or three hundred floors: you'd just swim. Over the sides of all the buildings, which were made in terraces, poured watery forests of leaning trees, and cascading creepers, vines, and flowers. Right around this window wall tumbled a vast vine that had roped some huge sort of seaweed trees. Blue, purple, and green grapes hung there, with a very large, black octopus feeding on them.

Otis and I moved away from the window fast. The audience chamber was packed with glamorous people, all white robes and dresses and undersea-type jewelry and hair done by the best hairstylists. Then a trumpet sounded (I think it was a trumpet, could have been an elephant for all I knew), and there was silence. And in came the queen, who sat on a marble throne.

Aragon is right.

She's stunning.

Check: raven black hair, which coiled around her, moving only a little in the water when she did. Check: creamy skin.

One of the I-suppose-damsels who were handmaidens murmured to me, "Of course you are made speechless by the queen's beauty and magnificence. But you must bow to her."

So I bowed.

And Bekmira Ren gazed at me, not even blinking her gold-painted eyelids.

Then she spoke.

She had this voice, sort of soft and harsh at the same time.

"There is no need for you to fear me, child," she said. (*Child* again.) "Providing you are honest."

"Say, 'No, Majesty,'" advised the handmaiden.

"No, Majesty."

"Good." Bekmira Ren lifted her hand and beckoned me forward. The water rippled; her sleeve floated a little, too.

Was I scared? No. But she was a bit—well, she was impressive.

I went over until I was quite near. (Check: her eyes *are* violet. Does she wear contacts? I've never seen real-color eyes like that.)

"Where are you from, child?"

It was no use getting upset over the "child" stuff. And I knew my lines now. "From the other world, Majesty." I decided against saying, *Like you are supposed to be, too.* Helpfully, I added, "My name is Jet."

"A fair name. I have a ring with a black stone like that in it. Well," she said, "you may go now. But in one hour you will be brought to my private apartments. There I shall question you further."

Just then the octopus, which I hadn't seen swimming up behind me, came into sight and put about ten of its million awful arms around Otis. I leaped forward with a yell. But she spoke again. "Crar. Let go the hound, Crar," she said. And Crar—the octopus—let Otis go and wafted up to Bekmira and curled up on her lap, with its slippery edges and lots of arms trailing down over her golden skirt. She stroked it. No accounting for tastes.

OTIS'S DISKRIPT: Anagram Reference

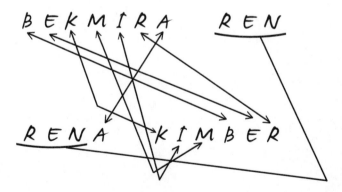

7

THE SURPRISE: EXTRA SCENE

Turquoise has another early start today, and as usual has gotten into the car that takes her to soundstages 90 to 101, where today's shooting of the *Fall of Super Troy* is scheduled. The earthclocktime is six-thirty (A.M.), because Turquoise must spend two hours in preparation and makeup. (In Reck Pandion's movies, these things are always done in areas close to the site of filming.)

Turquoise sits in the slinko drinking sparkling water and red grape juice, murmuring her important lines over and over. *"Yes, lady,"* murmurs Turquoise, putting herself into it. She is Ariasta, Third Damsel of Helenet. And she shares a scene today with the very hot Bat Temperance—even if, during this scene, they don't exchange a word or a look.

"*Yes*, lady—Yes, *lady—Aaah!*" screams Ariasta-Turquoise. "How—Where—*How did you get in this car?*"

Her sister Jet, and Jet's S.C. Deluxe dog, look at Turquoise, smiling. *Both* of them.

They are still decorated with jam, pancake, and juice. And three seconds earlier they were *not* in the car.

Nor has the car stopped, let alone opened any of its doors to allow them to enter. The car had been and still is speeding along the Avenue of Classic Black-and-White Footage. The driver is a machine, of course. So Turquoise banging on the window and yelling at it isn't making any difference. So far as the machine's (normally exquisite) senses tell it, both it and its passenger are fine. On it drives, and sticky Jet and Otis go on sitting and grinning.

Turquoise tries to think calmly.

Her horrible sister and the dog must somehow have hidden themselves in here (though how and where is a mystery).

"What do you want?" demands Turquoise. "Didn't you cause enough trouble back in the room?"

"Sure," says Jet. "For then."

Otis barks.

The bark goes right through Turquoise's head.

She screams: "The minute we get there you go away— you hear?"

"Sure, Turkey."

"Don't call me that, you little brat!"

"Turkey-lurky is a jerky!"

Turquoise starts to tear her hair, remembers her hair now belongs to *FOST* (and Reck Pandion), and leaves it alone.

After what Turquoise believes is a special personalized hell lasting twelve more minutes, the car slides to its preprogrammed halt by the entrance to soundstages 90 to 101.

The door opens.

Jet and Otis scramble out and start to dance around on the sidewalk.

Turquoise stalks by them, but, at the last instant, just as she touches the ID panel and the glass-steel doors, recognizing her print, are opening wide to let her in—Jet and Otis bound in past her, nearly knocking her down.

Turquoise screams yet again, and her juice and water bottles fall from her hands to smash (they are fashionable *old* glass) on the foyer floor.

Furious-looking robo-cleaners burst from the walls to tidy the mess.

Turquoise's personal exec steps from the elevator. "Hi, Turquoise, darling—Eek!"

In horror both exec and Turquoise watch as Jet and Otis sprint into the elevator, seeming to move faster than light.

"Call Security!" scream-practiced Turquoise screams.

The exec presses a button on her collar.

But the doors are shut, and right then the elevator takes off again. Jet and Otis are being whirled upward seventy floors.

When the elevator doors undo again, girl and dog leap out. They have now arrived in the foyer of soundstage 90.

There are juice bars, coffee bars, miles of rest and refurbishment rooms. There is also robot Security, which, strangely, doesn't react to Jet and Otis.

Beyond a soundproofed archway lies the second area of foyer, which leads directly onto the first stage.

Barely visible through the reinforced barrier, gigantic Magni Overcameras tower like alien life-forms from Earth Mars.

The archway doors open.

Out comes Reck, talking kindly to a fretful Bronze Shunk (who had a bad argument last night with Crimson Jones).

"Women," says Reck. "You have to let them do the work to get over it."

"Hi," says Jet, appearing before both men.

"Rwuff!" agrees Otis, and gladly flings himself directly at Bronze, who, despite his muscles, nearly falls flat on his back.

"Whose goddamn mutt is this?"

"Mine," says Jet. "I'm Turquoise and Amber's sister. They said you wouldn't mind if I come watch the shoot, huh?"

"The hell they did." Reck seems unthrilled. *No* one gets on his soundstage unless he says so. Did he? He thinks not.

And what on earth is that in this Jet kid's hair—*maple syrup*?

"In fact, n—" begins Reck.

"Gee thanks, Mr. Pantyhose!" gushes Jet, and rushes on through the second foyer into the stage area. Otis, using Bronze as a launchpad, and giving him a good kick in the jaw with a metal-reinforced hind leg, gallops after her.

"Shit," observes Reck.

"Ah shink de darn musht brook a toosh—" confides Bronze.

DIAMOND CITY: MONTAGE

Beautiful, drowned, ancient city, its terraces swallowed by high seas several hundred years ago.

Buildings have been built up higher by the Sea People. Mansions, temples, towers.

Gardens "hang" over carved balconies, terraces of columns, statues, roofs, lush deep emerald green, and with fiery corals, sea anemones, flowers, and ripe fruits.

Fish and small sharks, and little white whales, swim everywhere.

Brief but intense images:

On the lower avenues chariots race along, drawn by sea creatures—large fish, dolphins. Elegant people sit and drink wine amid gardens of roses. In a temple a weird old priestess performs some ceremony, throwing colored shells to form patterns, reading their meaning, while fish flit through the water-air. The priestess finally bows her gray-haired head and picks up one of the shells, which now has a tiny flame burning on it. The priestess shakes her ragged locks.

From high up, the general plan of the city is clear. From farther in, its richness is inspiring. No slums exist. Everyone seems wealthy, healthy, and good-looking.

And there are dragons, too.

Look up. What is that? A bird . . . a plane . . . a *cloud*?

A vast blue dragon spangles by, far above the tallest building, wings spread. It breathes out, through the bluer water, clear green waterspouts. It barely glances at the city below.

Now night is falling on the land above the sea, and so through into the watery kingdom darkness also descends. Lamps fire up in all the windows.

We reach the palace of Bekmira Ren, set on one of the highest points of the city. Swiftly we coast about its splendors—carvings, angles, gargoyles—and then pan in on one particular glowing window: within, the apartments of the queen.

Jet's Journal (*cont.* VOD)

Was I bothered about meeting her again? You bet.

Her rooms open off lamp-lit gardens with *eels* swimming through them.

She was being made up for the evening.

Damsels swam to and fro with trays of cosmetics and nail polish. Two were putting what looked like glowworms in her hair . . . The creepy octopus lay asleep on a chair, most of its legs dangling.

Bekmira Ren, AKA Rena Kimber, the vanished actress from all those years ago. "Now," she said to me, "you will tell me why you are here."

"I didn't *ask* to come here—some of your people *kidnapped* me," I replied indignantly.

"Naturally," she said. "I had sensed your presence in the upper land." She waved all the attendants away. If anything, she looked even more beautiful than before, so I guessed the makeup session was over. "I mean, why are you in this world?"

"Search me."

"There is always," she said, "a reason. Meanwhile," she added, "on land you were in the company with my great enemy, Aragon, Lord of the Forest People. He fought to save you from my men. They ran from him, too, because he is a fierce and brave warrior. If you refuse to speak of your own quest, you had better tell me what you know of *him*."

Uh-oh. You could see it in her eyes.

He liked her. But *she*—she liked *him*.

And let's face it, all either of them wanted to talk about, or hear about, was the other one.

"So right," I said, "you saw him face-to-face on a ship, in battle."

"He was captured but later cunningly escaped us. But in those moments when first we had him, I might easily have killed him." She paused, thinking about this.

"But you, er, didn't."

She stood up and clapped her hands, and all the damsels darted away out the room and the doors were shut. Now we were alone but for the odd fish and the octopus.

"I will confess to you," she sighed, staring at her eely garden. "No blow was struck—yet the sword entered my heart."

Here we went again.

"It is shameful that I love him," she said angrily. "I will have him captured one day, brought here as my prisoner, and slain. I shall teach myself to hate him. If needful, I will kill him myself."

"Sure."

"Oh, I can do it. My will is tempered steel. The water dragons are my beasts; I rule them. They swim beside my galley when we ride above the sea. Do you think such a woman as I, who can rule *dragons*, cannot rule her own heart?"

She was as annoying as Glorianne Bowsky in third grade.

"Why do you *want* to kill him?"

"We are sworn enemies," she said. Stupid.

"Can't you *un*swear it?"

Then, to my total fright, she marched up to me and

stood about a foot away. "You and I, Jet, come of the same people. I, like you, was human once. I barely recall it now. I lived in the outer world of shadows, where dreams never come true. I was named—"

"Rena Kimber," I couldn't resist blurting.

Her violet eyes widened. Then, she laughed.

"Oh, boy," said the Sea Queen Bekmira Ren. "Okay. You got me." And I had heard this voice, this second voice of hers, lower and more throaty, someplace else. "So fine, I'll tell you the deal."

"Do you want to stay here?"

"I . . . don't . . ." What could I say? *Did* I? Did I have a choice? "I haven't decided."

"You will. You won't want to leave Indigara. No one ever does. How'd it happen for you?"

She seemed to have forgotten her obsession with Aragon for the moment. She was really curious.

"There was a dragon in the Subway, and then some guys chased me, and one of the closed pipes opened—"

"Sucked you right in, yeah. Okay, here's the story. When I was up top, I made one movie, *The Wicked Couple.*

Ever see it? A really good film. But there was this other actress—not that she could act. She wanted my part, jealous as hell. Told a lot of lies. Gossip started. Lost my agent. Next contract got canceled. My whole career was ruined. So after a party in the Subway, I went off on my own to the tracks and waited. I won't tell you what I was planning to do. It was three in the morning, just after. They stop the trains between one A.M. and three. That's said to be a union thing, but it ain't. Oh, don't mind how I talk," she added, grinning at me. "I grew up sounding like this, and part of me still does." She patted Otis suddenly. Even he looked startled. "Eh, buddy? Well, that morning, the Subway clocks struck three *twice*."

"You mean it was six A.M.?"

"No. I mean three A.M. struck, and I glanced at my watch, which always kept good time 'cause my momma gave it me. And it was three, and a train came straight in along the tracks. But it came in real slow, no point in trying anything. So I stood there, and then I saw it was painted sea blue. And then the doors opened, and inside there was a sea blue dragon. I must have yelled. Maybe I couldn't. But I think it just scooped me up in one wing. And I had the strangest thought, that it was a water dragon because my birthday sign, back on Earth, would have been Scorpio, and my momma used to say it was a water sign. But then it was all scales and rushing and then there *was* water—and somehow I saw my watch, and it was still three, but I heard the clocks strike again three times, and I knew time had stopped but now time went on and I don't recollect another single thing until I woke up here, and I was the Queen of Diamond City."

"Queen Bekmira."

"Sure," she said. But she looked sort of sad.

And I thought, She wants to be here, but part of her wants to be . . . where she was, maybe. Part of her misses the real world.

Which must have been why I felt I had to say, "Well, anyhow, your enemy Aragon is so sweet on you he nearly made me sick."

She blinked. "Really?"

"Really."

And she smiled. She said, "Aragon O'Shane. Who'd have thought it. Not that he's the real Aragon, that guy never got in here. But looks just like he did in the movie."

For a minute then I realized that none of the times added up, because she had come into Indigara long ago, long before Aragon/Milsner had even *made* his movie, and even the movie itself—*Diamond City*—had been part of Indigara somehow *before* it was made. . . But then I thought of what she said about the clocks striking three twice and time stopping in between. I thought maybe time ran different here, maybe time didn't *matter* here. After all, it can't, can it, if you can go through a night in a couple of hours or a day in a couple of minutes?

This was when Otis spoke.

"Because everyone here is living in a pilot movie," said Otis, with a cool if slightly patronizing note, "the plot may turn out to be simple. Even ridiculous. But, too, it may have a plot-twist."

Becky gave him a long stare. "Oh, yeah? What does a robo-dog know? Hell, he talks like an old-Earth Boston butler."

Otis didn't lose his dignity. I could learn a lot from Otis.

He said: "Because your people snatched Jet, Aragon will have to attack you and your city at once. This is one of the oldest and perhaps most trite (at least, according to the critics) of plot devices: the brave yet vulnerable youngster who must be rescued, or avenged."

Becky changed at once. In her Bekmira voice she declared, as if to herself, "I must deny my heart's desire. I shall live only for my people. It is war. I will slay Aragon."

I glared at Otis. But Becky swept to her feet. She was all queen again. She stormed from the room.

As we followed her out, I hissed, "Now look what you've done! And, Otis—don't you *ever* call me a *youngster* again."

So it's war here. Great.

First they had a war feast, to which all the important courtiers came. They kept raising jewel-studded gold goblets and shouting about destroying things. And I apparently had to go, as I was Bekmira's valued guest, and symbol of the fact that she had treated me honorably, so the Forest People had no rights to me—well, it all sounded like garbage to me. I gave up listening.

Instead, I watched the feast, which was what you'd expect in an epic. There were endless plates heaved in

118

by staggering girls in gauze and staggering guys in kilts—staggering, I mean, under the weight of the food. It wasn't bad, but I'd have preferred a hamburger and salad.

When we got to the peacock-in-full-feather filled with what I think/hope/don't *like* to think was chicken liver pâté, wrestlers came in to entertain us.

There were several bouts, and if I hadn't been upset about the way things were going, I might have enjoyed it. Even underwater they were good, wrapping each other in headlocks and wristlocks and leglocks and throat-locks—or just by their long, flowing hairlocks if they came undone—and then throwing each other across the room and jumping on the fallen and bouncing until the one who was down gave in. No one seemed to get hurt, though sometimes they acted like they were. It was a great system.

I cheered up a little. Maybe *here* even a war could all be acting and pretense . . . couldn't it?

Finally the best wrestler arrived. He was called Thebennas.

All polished muscles, he threw his opponents to the floor and sat on them, and they were carried out in unconscious states that weren't quite convincing. But as he roared around, every time I glimpsed his face, I kept thinking I knew him from somewhere.

When he'd knocked out (maybe) ten men, the courtiers threw flowers and someone bellowed, "Just as the mighty Thebennas wins over all, so we win over all foes!" And spoiled it all.

But the queen beckoned Thebennas and gave him a ring off her finger, looking grave and wonderful and sad-but-I-will-not-weaken-ish. And then I saw Thebennas quite close.

When he straightened from his bow, he glanced right at me, too. And for one split second, he looked like he thought he might know me, too. But he turned and left the feast chamber without another look.

It wasn't the same as it had been when I saw Aragon. Aragon had been like Milsner, only he *wasn't* Milsner, just the character Milsner had played—and that character certainly didn't know me at all. But Thebennas— though a hundred times more fit and strong and ten years younger—was *Ben*: Ben who knew me, Ben from the Subway—*out there.*

Once Otis and I had gotten away from the feast, Otis showed me another diagram. The name Thebennas: Is the anagram of Ben's former stage name, Bennet Ash.

Yet Otis says Theb isn't actually Ben in quite that way . . .

Actually, what Otis says is, Thebennas is the *real* Ben, just as Becky is the *real* Rena Kimber. They are both human, and both here, acting the parts of the queen and the wrestler.

So who the heck—*what* the heck—was the "Ben" we met outside, in Studiocity?

Otis: "The Ben outside registered with me as human at the time. But I've mentioned about my not having my half-yearly check—"

"A couple hundred times, yes."

"Very well. I let you down. The Ben we met wasn't human, but he was very convincing. I have no real idea of what he is, Jet. None. Except . . . I believe when a real living person, such as Rena Kimber, or Bennet Ash, enters Indigara, they leave a sort of echo—a sort of *shadow* of themselves behind them, outside, in the real world. A being that is like them—yet not. *Not*."

In our room they'd given us, it seemed dark. The lamp was low. I shivered. "So the first Ben was a *shadow*?"

Otis said nothing.

"Er, Otis," I said, "if that's the case, do you mean *we* left our shadows out there, too?"

And Otis still didn't answer.

About five minutes later we both turned around fast because someone was splashing violently in the window. Maybe it's the way people have to knock here, since none of the windows have glass.

It was the weird old woman again with raggy gray hair and the long robe. Now she balanced there and waved her arms at me. I gaped at her. But she shrilled, just like before, "Beware the dragon of fire!"—and then just dropped about five hundred stories down the city and out of sight. I peered out after her, but she'd already vanished. On the window ledge lay a little shell, with a little red flame burning on it. But even as I saw it, the flame popped and went out, and the shell disappeared.

PART THREE

STUDIOCITY: SET PIECE

On soundstage 90, Reck is rehearsing his actors in scene 900 of *FOST*. The set is a vast open square in a futurist type of quasi-classical city. The square is filled by milling chariots drawn by mechanical brass horses. Sun-bronzed actors shout loudly about some king called Hectron.

Third Damsel Ariasta (Turquoise) is standing with other damsels on a pillared platform behind the leading actress, who plays Helenet.

Other actors in the royal court garb of Super Troy—

black leather, plates of gilded armor, big boots—stand glowering. (One of them is Bat Temperance.)

Every so often the rehearsal stops. Execs and makeup artists rush in to check continuity, powder everyone's face, tweak curls and flounces, burnish up the horses, and spray clouds of fake nonallergenic dust.

All this has now gone on for two hours. That's normal. It is a Big Scene, and nothing must go wrong when the Overcameras roll. When finally in the can, this scene will last a whole ninety seconds.

Turquoise has a line in this scene.

She will say, "Yes, lady," to Helenet, after Helenet (the famous leading actress) has sadly moaned, "They are barbarians here."

Bat Temperance has not glanced at Turquoise today. Not even in the check-powder-tweak-burnish-spray intervals.

There is, too, another cause for her unease.

When Turquoise at last came out of makeup and reached the soundstage herself, there was no sign at all of her brat sister Jet and that dog. Nevertheless, Jet had gotten in here. Turquoise knows this since Reck had glared at Turquoise and said, "You *do not ask relatives*.

Someone will speak to you later." That has put Turquoise right off her part. She keeps forgetting her line. Is it: "Yes, lady?" Is it: "Oh yes, lady?" Or even only . . . "Lady?"

Damn Jet. Turquoise will kill her.

That there isn't any sign of her among the crowd of makeup carts, production execs, or ground crew below the set and the stage is more worrying than not. Turquoise has the forceful impression Jet is in here but has not been found and removed.

The rumor circulates, too, that Bronze Shunk has had to visit the Dream-Works Dental Parlor in the building. A dental cap has to be fitted. Luckily he isn't in Scene 900, but the next one. Yet this has upset Reck as well.

It is essential, therefore, when shooting starts that everything goes without a hitch.

And now it's time. The false sky above the square comes on, blooming blue with some small tasteful clouds. An unreal sun beams to create extra highlights and shadows.

The cameras roll forward. If anyone breathes too loudly now, they will get fired.

Frowning, Reck climbs a gantry, reaches his favorite camera, squints through the lens. Seems satisfied.

Like a great musical conductor, he raises his hand.

The mechanical voice booms: *"Take begins."*

Abruptly the square comes to complete life. What in the rehearsal was hammy and silly grows convincing.

The charioteers roar, and the princes fight their way magnificently through the crowd. Helenet puts her hand to her eyebrow, and Turquoise remembers her line, and all the delight and challenge of living in make-believe soars through everyone.

And exactly then . . .

Exactly in the forty-fifth central second of the ninety-second take . . .

They are balancing eye-catchingly on the rail of a chariot. They are in the center of the seconds and the center shot that every camera covers. Jet and Otis, larger than life.

And Reck sees Jet through the lens, and Jet sees Reck (his face frozen to concrete, her face alight with friendly joy). And Jet waves. And she calls in a voice worthy of a foghorn, "Hi, Mr. Panfried!"

After which Jet and Otis spring, and as they hurtle on, several charioteers plummet smack on their faces. Across the backs of brass horses skitter Jet and Otis.

Jet whoops joyfully, and Otis barks.

Right across the square—chariots and citizens veering away in terror—up onto the pillared platform they bound, knocking Bat Temperance nose over tailbone as they pass, as well as sending ten or eleven other minor princes ass-first in a long, long, toppling, howling dive.

Helenet wails in a dismay better than she's acted so far as Otis leaps into her arms. In slow motion she falls backward amid her damsels, who, failing to catch her, collapse in turn. Only one avoids this, number three, Ariasta-Turquoise. Instead, she attempts to grab hold of Otis, who turns and lovingly licks her face clean of all two hours' worth of makeup, before he runs her straight into one of the white marble pillars.

It isn't marble. It is part of the set. Perhaps it's really plaster, judging by the way it breaks into seven pieces, and fountains of floury white stuff gush from it. Turquoise and the fallen heap of flailing, screeching damsels-and-Helenet are instantly remade as white plaster snow women.

Reck is himself shrieking from the high camera.

Because of the detonations of pillar plaster, the blue

sky of Super Troy turns first a livid yellow and then a pukey black. A rain of metallic glue and splinters starts to fall gently.

A wild stampede is happening.

Two cameras crash down in showers of sparks, and camera operatives hurl to safety amid the makeup carts, which go clattering off up ramps, to tangle with skidding brass chariot horses.

Alarms honk and flash.

Fire extinguishers come on. Torrents of water pour down—on everything—except Jet and Otis. Who once more . . . seem to have disappeared.

Jet's Journal (*cont.* VOD)

Time is weird, too, under the sea. I knew it would have to be. The night after the war feast was about four hours long.

At dawn I woke up to see all these golden stars falling smoking down through the water onto the city. And then the queen's guards were rushing, and everyone appearing on roofs and balconies and cheering. The stars, when they settled—and some fell in the gardens outside our room—were glassy pods with fires smoldering in them, and apparently this is the signal they've been expecting from Aragon and the Forest People saying, Yes, we'd love to meet you in war—or, We want to invite you to this terrific war, RSVP, et cetera. Depending, obviously, on who issued the challenge first . . .

After that, the whole city was activity and excitement, even worse than last night. And then their ships started to assemble high up over the city, in the water-air.

Seen from below they're really beautiful, the ships. They're all galleys like *her* ship, with sails rigged up (that's what they say, "rigged up") and the oars all stuck out ready. They're all decorated, too, in gold and silver, and the sails are white or red. They kind of lie up there like big dark-glittering clouds. But if you swim over to have a closer look, the way I did, you can see war machines on the decks. They call them *ballistas*. They can throw rocks and sharp metal things or gobs of fire.

Dragons have come in, too. Her dragons, the water kind. They are all like that one we saw in the Subway on A7. They have horse-dog faces, bluish greenish scales. They breathe out gusts of water that flares green through the bluer sea and *ice* green through the greener sea. Down here that doesn't seem to do much. But I suppose, like the horrible ballistas, once they're *above* the sea they'll be like water cannon.

Troops pour up and down all the time, taking things to the ships.

Sometimes she appears on a high roof of the palace and graciously waves. She has on a designer gown of golden mail, and a gold helmet thing with trailing long green plumes, with her hair coiling out from under it.

I feel so uncomfortable. I keep asking myself if this really has been caused by me, by my arriving in Indigara and then being captured by her guards, and Aragon having to rescue me because I'm this movie-type, feisty, utterly stupid fool of a *youngster*.

And there's the bigger question, too, obviously: the thing I thought of yesterday. Do people get hurt here in a way—or is it acting? Do they get *killed*—or just get up again when that day's take is done?

One other thing, so petty I don't know why I mention it, is that mad priestess woman or whatever she is who keeps on jumping out of the bushes or from around a wall, surrounded by swarms of fish, and yelling at me:

132

"Beware the dragon of fire!" It's happened at least six times so far. Last time I said to her, reasonably, "If I saw a dragon of fire, I am hardly going to rush over and pet it, am I?" But that did no good because I can see her lurking over there in that seaweed tree right this minute, getting ready to rush over again.

In fact, I've made a decision. Think I made it while I was recording all this via Otis. We're going to escape. It may not even be that difficult. She hasn't noticed me since our chat last night. No one even brought me breakfast. So what's to stop me from just heading off up, finding Aragon, and saying, Look, here I am. Now you can cancel your very stupid war.

STUDIOCITY: NIGHT PIECE

"I INSIST," thunders Reck.

Dad, in the doorway of the hotel apartment, squares up. "Whatever damn thing she's done, she's my daughter."

In the main room Turquoise and Amber cling together in an unusual alliance of fear.

Mom has given up. She is sitting *knitting* on a couch, ignoring everybody. She seems to wear an unseen sign that reads: ABSOLUTELY *NOTHING* IS WRONG AT ALL.

The door to Jet's room stays firmly closed.

"Has anyone informed you," says Reck to Dad, "of what *happened* to my movie today? Five billion stollars' worth of damage. At a rough guess."

Dad gulps. You can hear it.

Amber starts to cry. Turquoise howls, "It's not our faults. It's that brat Jet!"

Jet's door opens right on cue.

Out she saunters, with Otis trotting at her side.

Reck Pandion stares. Then he strides past Dad, past Turquoise and Amber, and moves in on Jet.

"I'm glad you're here," he tells her loudly. "I have something to say to you."

"Hi again, Mr. Panda." Jet grins.

That is . . . if this *is* Jet.

Well, perhaps we can see it isn't. Jet doesn't behave like this. Nor, for that matter, does the real Otis behave like *this* Otis. This Otis is dumb . . . and dangerous. And now he bounds suddenly forward and does his favorite leaping maneuver, landing with his front paws up on Reck's shoulders, while the rest of Otis kind of dangles down Reck's body like a . . . well, like a doggie bag. Reck glares, and Otis smiles into his face.

And then Otis washes Reck's face with his huge, flapping, soaking-wet tongue that smells—unlike the original Otis's tongue—of *cat* food.

And cut to—

INDIGARA: NIGHT: BATTLE LINES

Darkness is falling over the surface of the ocean.

We see Aragon's fleet like islands, ghostly in the dusk.

Pan across line on line of ships, as they wait there, their sails spread, their weaponry ready, the catapults and fire throwers in position. Torches are lighting. And smoke rises from offerings to strange Indigaran gods.

This land fleet Aragon has assembled is not only fewer in numbers than that of the Sea People, but duller and darker, less decorative than Bekmira's galleys. The ships look stolid and wooden, their sails of yellowish canvas.

We are close now, and we skim the decks, glimpse between hanging ropes and stretched stays, see teams of men oiling the war machines.

We reach Aragon's flagship.

They have lit lamps now in the prow, and Aragon stands there, dramatically lighted. He is magnificent, even if his armor is primitive. The sword is gripped in his hand. He is looking out. He knows, and now exchanges a few words with one of his warriors, saying that the enemy fleet will rise from the sea with the sun. The battle will be engaged at sunrise.

But then he is alone again. And we read clearly in his eyes that he is thinking of that enemy, that *beloved* enemy, and he murmurs softly, if only once, *"Ah, Bekmira..."*

But a sea fog is creeping in.

It muffles the ships.

Down in the water, there in the mist, something moves oddly. A fish?

Aragon half turns as he hears a slight sound behind him. Something emerges from the murk like a phantom— it is a man coming out of the fog. He is swathed in a dark cloak, and water drips from his garments and hair.

Aragon challenges him sharply.

The man shakes his head, and only holds out, in silence, a metal tube.

Aragon doesn't move.

The other man speaks. "If you call your men, Aragon, you will never read the letter this metal tube contains. See how easy it will be for me to toss it back over the side."

"Who sent you to me?" Aragon asks.

"Who do you think? Who do you think of the most?"

Aragon makes his decision, reaches out, and seizes the tube. He unscrews the top, and we see that it truly does contain a letter, which he unrolls and holds toward the light of the lamp in the prow.

The writing on the paper is this:

Ns slaa nll . . .

The subtitles appear, to reveal the message in English.

This war will slay both your people and mine.

Let us refuse war.

If you have the courage I believe you to have,

you will risk your fate and come to me alone.

You are a man and I am a woman.

Surely there can be more between us than battle?

Herewith, my seal:

BEKMIRA,

Ruler of the City

As Aragon stares at this, transfixed, we close in on the face of the sea-dripping stranger. He is shown to be the queen's chief wrestler, the powerful Thebennas. No sooner is that clear to us than Thebennas grabs Aragon by the throat. Thebennas applies one of the unconscious-making holds we have seen him use before at the feast. Aragon, despite his strength, can struggle only a moment before he collapses without a cry.

We pull back and back, away from the ship.

From some distance, and through the veils of the fog, we watch two shapes slide together over the side of the flagship, next sinking under the surface of the sea, then dropping swiftly into the depths below.

Jet's Journal (*cont.* VOD)

Otis and I had swum off a bit, away from all the black shapes of the overhead ships and cruising water-hissing dragons and the soldiers with torches diving around shouting, "Slay the enemy!" I got the idea they were going up to fight as soon as the morning light started to come down through the sea. And with the way time goes here, that could be in about twenty minutes.

I was trying to plan a way to go up through the sea, too, without . . . well, without fainting. Because Otis has figured out that is what happens if someone who isn't a Sea Person comes down through the water or goes up again. You black out. And I didn't want that, and anyhow, if that happened and a fight was about to start, I might get hurt, or at the best not wake up in time to try to stop it.

And I couldn't think of a thing.

Then we reached this sort of little cave place, with pillars and a lot of fish hanging around, and we just sort of glanced in, and—oh hell!—out flew that horrible woman with gray hair, and she was worse than ever.

"Beware—" she started off, of course.

"Of the dragon of fire," I helped out. "Sure. You've told me."

"No, no—" she caterwauled, adding some extra dialogue without warning. "You misunderstand me quite, dunce of a child! You are a daughter of fire. As the queen is water's daughter!" The new dialogue was so bad I lost the ability to say anything. So on she plowed. "Thus, thus, go you now and think not to evade your fate. For we are not your people. The fire is yours. Therefore, go!"

I was quite pleased to go, but the instant I turned back toward the palace, she came flailing after. "Fool! Fool! Beware the drag—" But luckily just then a whole squadron of soldiers came sailing down in their armor and pushed between her and Otis and me, and he and I fled.

And then I realized who the soldiers were hauling along in their grip, and he was passed out, too, and in chains—and it was Aragon—and right then they all went in one of the palace windows, and when Otis and I tried to follow, two big sharks came thrashing out like guard dogs. So Otis and I left the building.

THE QUEEN'S AUDIENCE CHAMBER

The chamber is full. The queen sits on her marble chair.

The prisoner, Aragon, Lord of the Forest People, is flung down before her, in his chains.

Bekmira speaks coldly.

"Revive him."

One of the guards slaps Aragon's face.

Aragon comes to and pushes himself, awkward in the chains, to his feet. But then he stands gloriously and faces the queen. "So," he says. "You have tricked me. You are the queen of spiders and have caught me in your web. More fool am I to have allowed it. What now? Here I am. I am ready to die. But let the innocent child go free."

(In fact, the innocent child, Jet Latter, has just wormed her way in at a side window. She and Otis regard the scene in a mixture of irritation and concern.)

"The innocent child," says Bekmira, "is already quite free. I have not kept her prisoner. It seems she prefers my city to your forest."

"It is my city also," says Aragon arrogantly. "You are a thief and a liar. Now I will trust you with nothing. Not even another word from my lips."

(A close-up of Aragon, and then Bekmira. Both look wonderful. All at once we see that *her* eyes are not hard or queenly. They glow brighter than the lamps.)

"Strike off the chains," she orders.

The guards protest, and the courtiers exclaim. But out of the crowd comes a huge man with the metal-reinforced tooth of a great whale. With this he strikes at Aragon's bonds, which fall crashing to the floor.

Aragon looks startled. So does everyone in the room,

apart from the huge man and the queen. (And actually Otis.)

Bekmira rises from her throne. She holds out her hands to the whole room, demanding its attention and obedience.

"I rule here," says Bekmira. "And this city is mine. But"—she pauses and looks at Aragon—"one other rules *me*. There he stands, my ruler. I love him, and without his love I am and shall be nothing. He has said he will not give me a single word from his lips. But I say this, People of the City. Either he shall rule with me here, or I will go away from this place. He and I shall rule you together, or he and I will rule in another place. His bravery and beauty are without question. Choose him as your king. And let him choose me as his wife. Or I shall leave you all forever."

Bekmira glides forward along the room and stands now in front of Aragon. Anyone who looks at them can see they are perfectly matched. Anyone can see they have eyes only for each other.

Now the close-up is only of the two of them.

"My lord," Bekmira whispers, "will you change your

mind, and after all give me the words of your lips?"

"I will give you my heart and my life," he softly tells her, "and the kisses of my lips instead of words."

Full close-up now as they embrace and their lips meet. Bring up music.

OUTTAKE

Jet scowls, and makes a gesture of putting her fingers down her throat in order to throw up. Otis blinks resignedly. He has been warned about this kind of behavior during S.C. Deluxe puppy training.

ADDITIONAL OUTTAKE

Queen Bekmira and Lord Aragon have entered the queen's private apartments. No one else is there. However, amid the lush furnishings, on a gold-plated table, with a base like a gold curving fishtail, stands a golden flagon that steams and has the definite scent of . . . coffee. A silver plate of fresh-baked doughnuts lies alongside.

"Oh, honey," says Bekmira tenderly, "I bet you've been dying to taste that coffee ever since last time, on that ship."

"I cannot deny it," Aragon answers. "Do you recall how we sat and drank it while the battle raged all about?"

"I sure do. Say, why don't you give me a second to fix my hair. That helmet totally ruined it. Kick your boots off and sit down."

Jet's Journal (*cont.* VOD)

Nights and days have whisked by. It's been like one of those old-fashioned disco lights. Bright, dark, bright, dark.

Settling down now. They are getting wed, Becky and Aragon. A big alliance. Both Forest and Sea Peoples, touched by their L-O-V-E, have come around to the idea. That's all right. Fine.

But it's really made me realize that I shouldn't be here.

I'd had a break from the old bat and her dragon-of-fire stuff. Then today, which went more slowly, dawn to dusk taking all of two whole hours, she jumped out of a window in the city, and we were off again: *Beware, beware* . . .

And then Ben, I mean Thebennas the wrestler, was standing right there, and he said to her, "She is missing some of what you tell her, priestess." And then, amazing me a bit, he added to me, "Jet, look, here is the subtitle."

By then the sunset had started, all rosy through the sea, but I could just make out the subtitles. And so I saw that what the priestess had been saying wasn't "Beware the dragon of fire." No, what she'd been saying (over and over and over) was, "Be *aware*—the dragon of fire."

I still didn't know what she meant, but it explained her awful going on and on about it, trying to make me see.

So I bowed to her and said, in my best Indigaran, "Pardon me, priestess. I thank you for your care."

And she gave a grunt. And then she swim-floated off. And Theb said, sounding ordinary, and like Ben, "We can sit on that gargoyle. And I'll spell it all out."

"The thing is, Jet, Otis," said Theb/Ben, "you've left a sort of shadow of you, back in Studiocity. We all have, Rena—Bekmira—and me, and the others . . . oh, sure, there've been more than just us. But—excuse me here, Jet, I know you are an adult young woman—but you're still pretty young. The rest of us, we were getting old, one way or another. I think Rena told you, her career was ruined, and she was thinking of throwing herself under the first fast Subway train. And me—well, I was lonely as

hell. We were all like that, all but you. And so the shadows
the rest of us left are kind of *quiet*. They know how to
go on in the real world; they keep their heads down and
play along. They are stuck—boring, kind of. Like people
can get if they haven't got much in their lives anymore.
But you . . . well. As they say, you have your life ahead
of you. So the shadow *you* left is a wild thing. And as for
Otis—that'll be even worse. I am sure Otis is gentleman
enough he won't get angry if I say he isn't even an animal.
So what kind of shadow dog did *Otis* leave behind?"

Otis and I sat there thinking about this. Otis turned on
the soft light in his eyes, and I leaned on him.

Ben/Theb continued: "People need to be upset and
desperate to get here. But maybe that feeling has passed
now for you? You have folks, something? Something you
want to do?"

"I guess," I muttered. Like when Becky-Rena had
said it, I wasn't sure either way if I preferred being here,
or there. The only thing was, I missed them. My family.
Missed them. *Worried* about them. And Indigara, though
it's so splendid and astonishing, just wasn't real.

Theb said, "The point is, those shadows of yours will

be causing real trouble out there. Because they are that different kind of wild, young, even *nonhuman* shadow. Think about this: they can appear and disappear how and when they want—just like all shadows. Though they look and feel real because they came out of us, a solid wall can't stop them, and the best security system, though it can see them, won't react. *But.* If you two go back, then the shadows lose their power. And they can't stay in the real world either, if you both are there instead."

I said, "So if I wanted to go back . . . how do I *do* it?"

"Shall I tell you," said Theb, "what the priestess meant about the dragon of fire?"

"Okay."

"It's your birth sign," said Theb. "That is, your birth sign if you'd been born on Earth. Your people are from there originally, right? So are all of us, in the beginning. Rena is Scorpio, that's a water sign. She even had a water dragon come bring her here. Mine is Aquarius; he's air. So my dragons, if I ever need them, are air dragons. But you are fire."

"Aries," I said. "Mom had an earth chart zodiac thing done for us all." I recalled Mom telling me about the chart and Aries, when I was about six. Aries is a sheep. A fiery sheep. Not something to which I'd normally proudly admit, frankly.

Above, fish sparkled through the now-nighttime water. Lamps gleamed from the terraced gardens and the graceful buildings, and above, all the ships and dragons were gone, because the war was off.

"So are you saying, Ben—er, Thebennas—if I want to go home I have to find a dragon of fire? Isn't that a little. . . dangerous?"

But he nodded.

Far below chariots drawn by sea beasts sped along streets, and I heard harps and songs, and it was lovely. . . and boring.

But I thought, This is going too fast now, like we're in the last fifteen minutes of the movie, when everything needs to speed up and happen.

And already Theb and I and Otis had drifted off the gargoyle and were swimming away from the palace, on the quest for this flaming dragon of mine.

Did Theb know where we were going? *I* didn't.

But.

You know, up there, out there, in the actual world, I felt I didn't have that much say in things. Mom'd say, *You should do this*, Jet. Or Dad would say, *Just do this*, *Jet*. Or some teacher would tell me I *had* to. Or Turkey or Amber would tell me if I *didn't* they would skin me alive. And, well . . . You grow up and you have to go to school and take classes and go to college and get good marks, and if any adult says you have to be someplace, or even travel someplace—like to Ollywood because your sister is in a movie—there isn't much choice. You have to. One way or another. But none of *that*—

Had ever been like *this*.

Like someone else wrote all the script, and all you could do in the end was . . . *act it out*.

But that is Indigara.

That's the price you pay for total, complete fantasy and dreams come true.

I've had some pretty scary dreams, you know. I prefer them to stay in my sleep. I don't *want* to live them out. Don't want my whole *life* written—*scripted*—for me.

STUDIOCITY: PLOT TWIST

"Listen, Jet," said Reck Pandion as Otis slobbered on his face, "you need to take this in."

"Fire away, Mr. Pandemic."

"What am I? I am a *risk* taker. I am a worlds-famous director *noted* for taking risks. Reckless Recktor Pandion. Today you ruined my picture. Today billions of stollars were lost. Do I go crazy? Do I doubt my genius?"

Everyone in the hotel apartment held his or her breath. Except Jet and Otis, the shadow demons who—if anyone had bothered to look properly—didn't cast a shadow. Just as, down in the Subway that night, Rena Kimber *Martha* didn't, nor Bennet Ash *Ben*.

"So what should I do, Jet?" asked Reck, blazing with powerful, confident faith in himself.

"You tell me, Mr. Pantechnicon."

"I scrap the idea of making one more tired old epic called *Fall of Super Troy.* Instead, I make the funniest damn movie anyone ever saw since Keaton and Chaplin and Laurel and Hardy and Steve Martin. I make *MAKING the Fall of Super Troy. The Fall of the Fall of Super Troy.*

I give them swords and sandals and Helenet and Shunk and a cast of millions, and I show sky exploding and columns falling and actors covered in plaster—and the audience is going to laugh themselves silly."

He's gazing up at the ceiling now. He doesn't notice the fine web of weed-guano that has formed up there. He doesn't even notice, so thrilled is Reck with his own inspiration and talent, that Jet and Otis have suddenly disappeared, like the best kind of special IT effect. Not, that is, till Amber screams and Turquoise screams and *Dad* screams—and then, as the cat-food doggie saliva dries on his unlicked face, Reck hears the click of Mom's knitting as she puts it carefully down. And Mom says firmly, "We must all just really try to stay *very serene*."

9

The fire dragon dwells in the depths of the ocean, deep in the crater of a subsea volcano.

The water here is darkest green, through which furl various weird fish (tendrils, fins like huge sails) and things like silvery manta rays, sting-laden jellies, and spined snakes. They are luminous and light up the sea.

Then a dull red glow begins.

We move in smoothly and hang above the smoking fiery crater. The fire flickers, now fierce, now dull, like a giant candle. A vague but disturbing rumbling roar sounds through the water. (In any world's sea, like in space, you can't hear anything much—certainly no one can hear you rumble. But Indigara's sea, of course, is an effect, and you can hear whatever you need to, if it moves things along.)

After the rumble, a kind of black shadow flicks up from the crater.

A wing?

Now we catch a couple of glimpses of something brazen, scaly—a flank, a jagged crest . . .

A spout of flame bursts from the hole.

It seems Mr. Fire Dragon is home.

OTIS'S DISKRIPT

More and more, since we have been in this place, I find all my inner files will give me are notes on movies, movie stars past and present, and supremistic effects.

Now I find a trailer for the original pilot *Race of the Dragons*.

There is a shot of one of the fire variety, in its lair.

Unreassuring.

Jet's Journal (*cont.* VOD)

It was getting darker, which might only have meant we'd gone to a lower depth. But really I thought something had just made the night sea extra black. Because, let's face it, a fire dragon would look its most dramatic that way.

I kept asking myself how a dragon could get me out of Indigara. But I remembered, too, that I'd seen a dragon in the Subway, and Becky's story of the dragon on the train, which grabbed her and brought her here, and the clocks striking three and time stopping and then three again . . .

Crazy fish everywhere. And some old ruins with seaweed on them, and leaning broken columns . . .

We reached a sort of cliff in the sea, and here there was more light, sort of like a green dusk. Theb pointed up.

And then this huge shadow covered us, and this huge darkness like a whole *planet* flew slowly over above.

I thought it was a water dragon. This, though—

"*Watch,*" said Theb.

And the dragon breathed out.

A sheer clear path cut right through the water.

"But it's—"

In the path was a wide gust of pale blue light and some little clouds, and two birds flew around.

"Air dragon," said Theb. "*They* breathe out air. And sometimes sky."

Gradually the air-sky part was melting away now. But the dragon still hovered above, turning its long face, which was like that of an eagle and had a big beak, down to us.

"Don't worry, Jet," said Theb. "He's friendly. He's mine."

What could I say? I kept quiet.

A last little puff of a cloud bubble, with the two birds in it, sailed off up toward the surface. The birds were relaxed, sitting on the cloud safe inside and preening.

And just then a low, grim rumble rocked through the water.

"That's about a mile off," commented Theb.

He meant the fire dragon?

The air dragon, meanwhile, had landed on the cliff top. Like the birds in the air bubble, it began to give itself a thorough preen.

Theb turned and swam off. So I did, and Otis. And now we were heading for the fire dragon, right?

And less than a minute later all the water went ink black and I could see nothing—and then worse than that. I began to see the scarlet glow up ahead.

I can remember when I was about eight and Amber was ten and Turquoise twelve, we all went to see a movie at Sensation Domerama. The movie had dragons in it. For about a month before, Amber kept on telling me I'd be so scared I'd be under the seat. But I liked it, and Amber was the one who kept squeaking and hiding her face in Mom's shoulder.

She would *really* have had super-hysterics if she'd seen what came out of that crater.

Otis did something like he'd have done out in the real world, only now I wasn't sure it wasn't just what the "script" made him do. He defendingly sprang in front of me.

We'd reached a kind of pebbly beach, and Theb was standing ahead of us, nearest to the flaming red-gold of the crater, which gaped in the blackness. Only dragon fire lit the scene. Theb looked like he was made of brass and Otis of furry steel.

Mostly I just had eyes for the dragon.

It *crawled* up out of the crater, and the fire glow spilled out with it.

Of all the dragons I'd seen, it was the most thin and sharp-edged. It looked as if it had been cut from metal. It crept and crawled, but not because it was taking care. It was like a cat creeps after a mouse. And we were the mice . . .

The water dragon has a face like a kind of horse-dog, and the air dragon is like an eagle, and the earth dragon is like a snake. The dragon from the fire has a face like a lion—but scaled. From its jaws curled this tiny wisp of smoke, like a delicate crimson scarf. That was all. It was enough.

I was so scared I *wasn't*. I didn't feel a thing. It was like nothing mattered. I *couldn't* have run or swum away. I'd changed to stone.

But then the dragon swung its head around, and it stared right at me. Yeah, it was . . . personal. It had golden stars for eyes. Inside its scaly skin it seemed only full of flames.

And then it did that sneeze thing the earth dragons did in the forest—started to gasp in its breath—and I knew this "sneeze" would be *fire*—

"Ben!" I shrieked.

I *did* shriek. I'm not going to apologize.

And I'd gotten his name wrong.

But he knew. He had raised his hand and from no-where, or rather out of the dark of the Indigaran ocean, something came rushing like a huge wave.

And then the fire dragon sneezed, or breathed out—and, as the scarlet fire bellowed out, something else gushed to meet it through the water. It was palest dusk blue, and full of clouds—and spangly stars now—and I saw the air dragon was up there behind us and it was puffing out and out over our heads, and straight at the fire dragon, air and evening sky and stars. And as the red fire exploded, the air hit the fire and—

The fire—

Ever blown out a match or a candle?

The air-breath blew out the fire-breath. *Whoosh*. Like that. All that was left were a thousand little embers float-ing and sizzling and fading, and some purple smoke that smelled of bonfires in fall.

I thought, idiotically, The sky the air dragon blew was dusk sky, but it must already have been night up there on the land. And maybe the blown-out sky only had to be pale to make it more effective-looking . . .

And then I sat down on the beach; I didn't mean to, just found I had. Otis stared at me and searched my face with his softest-lit eyes.

But Theb announced, "Water doesn't put out fire here. And you'd get a lot of scalding steam besides if one of the water dragons blew on the flames. But air . . . well. You've seen."

The air dragon drifted quietly above. The last pale blue was going out. The fire dragon glared up and raked the stones with a huge, scaled, clawy forefoot.

"Bonus," said Theb. "Once their fire's blown out, takes them a while to recharge. Around half an hour when I timed it last." And then, his voice really excited, he said, "Hey, look who I just found." Completely brainless, I gazed where he pointed. "See that? That's my Dusty from the robo-gang." Theb had obviously gone nuts. Then I saw a little Studiocity cleaning machine half buried in the stones. It was, must be, the one Ben had lost in the Subway, just before we saw the dragon up there and all this started. Theb was already busy hauling Dusty out of the ocean floor. "Even some machines prefer it in here," he said. "Up you come. But also the dragons—well, you may have read on Earth they were meant to have hoards of treasure. Our kind here seem to gather hoards, too, and sometimes they pick little critters like Dusty." Dusty now stood on the pebbles. It gave a little twitter, and went scurrying off, its dusting mechanism polishing up the stones.

Theb watched, and smiled. He said, "In fact, Jet, now is the time to make your move. I said about half an hour before your dragon gets his furnace going again. You've got only about twenty-five minutes now."

I jumped up. I said, "But what do I—"

A move. On a dragon. And it was growling like a lion now, too. No fire came out. There was that.

And then it shook its head, and the growling stopped. It lowered its back end to the pebbles and sat there. It looked over again, all casual. No doubt it was just deciding it could, after all, just eat us—me—raw. I'd be cooked inside it later, once the fire came back on.

"What do I do?"

"Okay. Swim straight over and up onto its neck. Sit just behind the crest. Otis, too. And both of you hold on tight.

160

I mean, *tight*. The scales there make good hand—and tooth—holds."

I said, "Wow. That easy. And then? I mean before it kills me?"

"It won't. Trust me. Here is the magic formula. You just say, loud enough it can hear, 'You want a doughnut?'"

"I say *WHAT*?"

Theb repeated patiently, in his other voice, "'You want a doughnut?'"

"But—"

"They've been spoiled, Jet. They don't like eating people. They like *takeout*."

"T-t-take—"

"Blame it on Rena," he said. "It started with her water dragons, but word must've gotten around. They all like the wrong food now. And they have found a way to get back into the Subway and out again so they can get it. Rena's dragons bring some in for her, too. You would be surprised those of us at Bekmira Ren's court who drink coffee. And the dragons are like raccoons on Earth; they've gotten to prefer what's in the human garbage. Sad but true."

Otis said, "Jet, ten minutes of the half hour are up now."

I started off before I knew I was going to.

I ran and swam with Otis at my side, heading right for the fire dragon, and before I knew how stupid I'd been, we were splashing right by its terrible face, straight by one huge gold eye that blinked one scaled lid, and the long black dragon tongue whipped from its great mouth stuffed with enormous pointed teeth—and we had gotten behind it; we were up on its neck behind the crest, and I yelled at the top of my voice, "HEY, WANNA DOUGHNUT?"

And the dragon . . . sighed.

Its breath smelled sweet. Like fresh biscuits.

Otis had sunk his teeth into a scale and closed them. I took a firm hold with both hands. The dragon took no notice of this.

It was heaving itself upward.

Below, Theb on the pebbles. His air dragon had settled a way off, grazing on some seaweed.

And with no warning my dragon took flight.

For a moment I thought we'd be shaken off, but Otis's grip held—and so did mine. If any of it had been really real I don't think that would have been possible. So it must have been one more direction in the script . . .

Theb and even the air dragon grew as small as the pebbles on the seafloor. Then they vanished. We were rising more slowly now, the wing beat steady, like the great scything slaps of a pair of huge blown shutters.

Suddenly, far off, miles and miles away in the core of the sea, I caught sight of the miniature gleams of what must be Diamond City. The lamps and torches were like the tiniest sequins scattered over the dark toy terraces, gardens, towers. An emerald luminescence shone around. It was a wide-angle lens model shot, I guess.

And it was somehow sad; it was somehow beautiful and sad and vulnerable and *wonderful*—like they say it is, if you see any world from outer space.

And then I fell asleep.

In all the stress I'd forgotten about that losing consciousness thing. But this wasn't like the abrupt blackout that happened before. Somehow I knew that, even like this, I and Otis wouldn't let go. It would be okay. It was . . . written that way. In fact, you know, I think the passing out—the sleeping—is just a kind of . . . edit.

- - - - - - -

When we woke up again, we were still in place, and just rising clear of the star-sparkly sea. We were flying in the night sky of Indigara, into the airspace over those great forests.

There was still no moon. But the stars were bright, and there were lots and lots of them. I saw the dragon's shadow thrown down blacker black on the tops of the trees a couple of hundred feet below.

Now and then a faint hint of village fires showed through the forests, but the dragon took no notice of them. There was a river once, too, winding and curving like a dragon's tail.

Little gauzes of red smoke had begun to uncurl from my dragon's jaws but no fire. The smoke smelled of hot cookies. And then more of *burnt* cookies. The fireless half hour must be nearly up.

"Doughnut," I bawled encouragingly.

But all this was insane. I was sitting on a *dragon*. And where was it going? And how the hell could it get back into the outer world? And I thought even if *it* could—could *I* really get back there? However real it seemed, the dragon was a computer effect. I was flesh and blood, and Otis was even more solid than I was. Made me feel nauseous. Supposing we kind of hit the barrier and *stuck*?

But neither Otis nor I fit in Indigara. We weren't like any of the others who had escaped into it. And so maybe Indigara would be glad to deport us . . .

Oh. The dragon was beginning slowly to circle around and around.

It moved in a wide sweep, the slap-slap of the wings now sounding like a huge tarpaulin left out in a gale.

Around and around, and below the forests and above the stars and then . . .

A kind of circular towerlike shape began to appear at the center of the circle, which *hadn't* been there, though the dragon had been circling it. And the more the dragon circled the tower shape, the more dense and non-see-through and black it became. It stretched right down into the heart of the forests below. It stretched right up and vanished into the heart of the sky overhead. And where it was it now shut out the view of stars or trees. And abruptly I knew what it must be. It was one of the big pipes that run from Studiocity through the Subway to the libraries and stores and archives under Ollywood.

And I was very desperate suddenly and shouted at the dragon's spiky ear, *"Doughnut! Doughnut!"* And Otis was barking, and then there was something burning in the pipe, a red light going on and off. The dragon gave a snort. Folding its wings and sticking its head on its long neck forward, it dived straight at the light, and into the light, and Indigara was going, going . . .

G O N E.

OTIS'S DISKRIPT

The dark alley had the street name of B19, and was lit by flashing red neon at the back of a restaurant. The dragon's mouth also flashed red as it sat smokily devouring dumplings, bean sprouts, and ginger chicken from a large dinner pail. How it had gotten this meal I had not seen. The food was simply there.

Jet stood beside me.

I felt I couldn't move, and Jet, too, seemed frozen.

And then hundreds of clocks of all types struck three. My legs twitched and I shook myself, and Jet did the same thing, but in a human way.

We were in the Subway. Up the alley, an unpainted closed pipe passed down through the street. Through this pipe we had been returned to reality.

"Otis," said Jet very softly, "let's get out of here."

We certainly moved then. We pelted out of alley B19, and along others called B18 and B18B and B17, and then we came out in a maze of Subway streets that had the usual overhead parasol lamps and baskets of fake flowers. All the streets were deserted, and all the stores here were shut.

We ran on for a while, and had emerged from Avenue Ridley Scott, next tearing down the sidewalk to the corner of Olivier's *Hamlet* and Coppola's *Dracula*, when all the clocks struck three again.

Jet stopped dead. I did, too.

In the silence after the clocks, something sinisterly dragon rumbled deep in the ground. Yet this was only a train coming in along the tracks.

A moment later Jet gripped me by one ear. This is a thing she has seldom done since she was nine. "Otis—*look*!"

And, indeed, I did look. For up Coppola's *Dracula* a pair of familiar figures were running toward us. A girl with black hair and an S.C. Deluxe dog. They, too, were Jet and Otis.

10

Jet's Journal (Usual Transcript)

She looked at me.

I looked at her. Or—at me.

I guess she was me. Not what I'd see in a mirror. But what I've seen in a photo, or home movie . . .

Jet.

Okay.

"Hi," I said.

And then *she* said, "Yeah."

Otis said nothing. And the other dog—*Otis*—said nothing. He is *not* like Otis. Oh sure, to look at—but he isn't smart like Otis. He's like a proper S.C. Deluxe, maybe without all the training. But Otis, even if he did make a couple of mistakes, is *Otis*. (And this other Otis had raspberry jam in his fur. Yuck. Come to think of it, so had she, for God's sake.)

They were our shadows.

The ones who had behaved in this wild, trouble-causing way Ben had suggested.

They looked like they would have.

The lights were brighter and the trains were running, but it was so early in the morning that none of the stores were open yet. You could sense people waking up, the ones roomed in the Subway. You could feel the Subway itself waking up. And then across the end of Coppola's *Dracula* some guys passed with a robo-cart, and headed off down into the station to load up a train.

Real life was coming back.

But Jet 2 and I just kept looking at each other. And I thought, Aside from the jam, is my hair *really* that rotten? And then she did speak.

"I've done a couple of things out here, Jet."

"Have you, Jet."

"Uh-hah. Just a bit of messing around. What you'd have *liked* to do. If you'd had the guts. Or the clever ideas."

My heart banged. I said, "You didn't kill anyone?"

"Nah. Don't be a dope. I'm a piece of you, Jet. I don't want to kill . . . I only want to get even."

"Sure."

"Oh, don't start that sure stuff with me. I'm *you*, remember. I got created when you went into the dream world."

"Indi—"

"—gara. Yeah. Only you didn't have the brains to stay there, did you?"

I felt truly peculiar. It wasn't that I was talking to me. It was what *me* said to. . . *me*.

I blurted, "There wasn't enough in Indigara—or too much—and it wasn't right. I was bored—I was—I don't know . . . and I missed—"

"Mom," said Jet 2 in a mocking, babyish whine. She laughed. She doesn't have my laugh. "And you missed Daddy and Turquoise-y the Turkey and Amber-y the Pain. Miss *them*? You are cracked."

"Yes, I guess I am."

"But that doesn't matter," she said. And right then she sprang forward and Otis—*my* Otis—growled like the lion dragon, but the other Otis—*hers*—just sat there panting and grinning. She didn't pay any attention to either of them. She was now just inches from me. "I," she said, "was made when you went into Indigara. I kind of split off from you. It's the energy that sparks up when that happens that makes it possible. And it's balance. If you are *there*, then something that's you has to be *here*. But I won't blind you with science. Now you've come back, so I can't stay here, too. And that is just great by me. I don't *want* to stay out here. I bet you are wondering, *How does she even know about Indigara if she has only been out here?* I know because *you* know. The same way I know your whole life. But you, Jetty, don't really know a single thing about me. That isn't going to matter. You are back, so I am free to go. *You* can deal with your stupid family now and all this twits-ville world. *I*, and my *dog*, will go instead, and are going, to Indigara, where dreams come true. Say, Jet, you moron, don't you even know Indigara was what you really wanted? To grow up fast and be a queen and rule the place. Yeah, you wanted that so bad, how else did it let you in? But

172

you're just a stupid kid, and you wouldn't face up to what you wanted. How else did Indigara *let you go*?"

I couldn't think. Then I did. "But if I'd wanted it I would have *faced* it. And stayed."

"No," she said. "You know, I bet you secretly thought you weren't good enough for Indigara. And maybe *you* weren't."

She sounded older to me. And then . . .

Then she really was older than me.

It was like those effects in movies when someone changes into a monster, or gets younger, or older.

Basically Jet—I—grew up in front of me.

Right there. On Coppola's *Dracula*, before the stores opened.

She got taller, and though she didn't get much fatter, she kind of filled out. She had—I have to say—a really good figure. Like she ate right and exercised, but also like she had it naturally anyhow. And her hair was clean and styled and shiny, and her face—*my* face—she had become good-looking and cool and strong. She looked great. I—I looked . . . I looked great.

"I'm sixteen now," said Jet 2. Said me. "I am a bitch

on wheels. I'm going to live in Indigara and ride the dragons of fire. All of them. I'll make them all mine. I'll get
around Bekmira. I'll be a better queen than she is. And
Aragon? Oh, I'll get him, too, you see if I don't. I tell you,
Jet, even if no one ever sees this, it's going to be one of
the best movie sequels ever made. Right, Otis?" Her S.C.
Deluxe dog barked. "Otis and I," she told me, "are going
to conquer the world."

I believed her.

And then she and the dog jumped, and they were up
in the air over my head, which was when the fire dragon
came sweeping back on jagged wings, smelling now of
scorched Chinese takeout and burned pizza. It swooped
low and sailed beneath them both, and there they were,
the girl and her dog, sitting up on its back. And the
dragon carried them away with the rushing roar of a great
wind, over the buildings to where the nearest closed pipe
ran down. It was painted with images of the classic old
film *V for Vendetta*, but the images all gave way on a
living scene of Indigara's dark blue night. Into the gap
the dragon went, with Jet 2 and Otis 2. I saw them all fly

toward the forests and the sea. And then the break in the pipe was sealed once more.

When I looked around, Otis had his strongest eye light on.

"She was full of it," I told him.

And my Otis nodded his head, then wagged his tail.

PART FOUR

PART FOUR

11

STUDIOCITY: LOSING THE PLOT: EDITS

The elevator is empty from Studiocity to the Subway, though at the top there are already crowds of people waiting to ride down and start the working day. It is about five A.M. earthclocktime.

When Jet emerges above onto the Boulevard of Overnight Success, everything is caught in an ordinary pink-gray dawn, through which already crews and machines are moving, and here and there half-made sets trundle by on auto-sleds, segments of ancient Rome, or

New Mars. She passes a couple of stalled sleds, too, with men swearing and pushing buttons.

Jet notices almost at once how much weed-guano has grown along the sidewalks, up the sides of lots, along the wide avenues and semiclassic buildings. In the trees, palms, pines, and cedars, the weed is strung about like nets. Clearing machines and robo-fixits are squirreling everyplace, trying to mop it up, hack it off, pull it free.

In the sky, a little lumpy mechanical cloud crosses sluggishly. It trails a smoke plume that reads: *WEL O E WO L F M IC—OYOO.*

Puzzled, Jet mentions this to Otis.

Otis finds he can work out that what the smoke plume should say is, WELCOME TO THE WORLD OF MAGIC—OLLYWOOD.

He is pleased by this, since it seems to mean he is functioning better. Also, now, not every word he speaks seems pre-written, which it had. He assumes Jet feels this, too.

He is also aware, however, that meeting her other self has unnerved Jet.

Otis and Jet jog along the boulevard, where some very large cracks are being repaired in the roadway.

Finally they see the top of the swan hotel.

Both girl and dog gaze up in awe.

Almost the entire hotel has been smothered in weed-guano. Just here and there a hole has been left or ripped free. Only the head, with the banquet-ballroom, pokes out, looking bewildered.

Hundreds of robo-flyers are at work all over the swan, tearing and blasting at the weed.

On the ground are various emergency crews. Everyone seems to be busily getting nowhere.

Jet's Journal

We were stopped by the electrostat cordon at the hotel entrance.

"Hey, hey, young lady, not so fast. You can't go in there."

The burly man in uniform glared down at me, but I'd dealt with a takeout-hooked fire dragon—a fire chief was nothing.

I said, "My mother and dad are in there."

"No one's in there. Whole place was evacuated."

"Where are they, then?"

"Depends who they are and who they know."

"My sister is in Reck Pandion's movie."

"Right? Okay. Hey, Elvis," called the fire chief to one of his men, "know where the top actors' families went?"

"Washington Square, Jedi Hotel," said Elvis.

"Jedi Hotel in Washington Square," explained the FC to me, as if I had to have it translated. With which they both walked off to inspect something.

I didn't know where the square was, but Otis thought he could find it; his normal files were coming back.

In the end we didn't have to search. As we raced along a side street five minutes later, a huge car swarmed past me. Thought I recognized it, then I did. It was the slinkousine that took Turquoise to the studio each day. Right then it pulled up and the rear door slid open.

"It *is* you, you little ugly messy creep!" lovingly screeched Turquoise as she craned out.

"Messy and ugly, huh?" I asked. "Seen yourself lately?"

And for once it was absolutely a fact.

Whatever else my oldest sister is or isn't, she is not ever ugly or, since coming to Ollywood, a mess. At least . . . not till today.

"Okay, wiseass. Get in the damn car!"

So I did. I was thinking the family were probably together now, after the hotel problem, and so I'd find Mom and Dad quicker if I stuck with Ariasta. But also I kind of wanted to feast my eyes on her, too.

Her hair was powdery white and stuck out all over the place. Her face was without makeup and, instead, smeared thickly with more white, and also some black, goo, and various crumbs and tufts. Her dress was in ribbons and covered—like every other spare inch you could see of her— with caked-on muck of a selection of colors and textures.

"So what happened to you?" I asked her, kindly. "Let me guess—you fell in a cake mix in a sewer."

"You *pest*! It's all your *fault*. That . . . *stunt* you pulled, and that disappearing trick—he thinks you're a *genius*. He thinks you're his *muse*—"

"*Who* thinks? *Muse*? What's a mu—"

"You ignorant rat. His *inspiration*. He keeps saying, 'Whichever of you finds me that brilliant golden girl will earn my undying gratitude.'"

"The golden girl is me, right? So you're so lucky. You found me."

She made a noise that reminded me of the fire dragon.

But my mind ticked, like a time bomb. I glanced at Otis. I said, "Turquoise, have you ever thought everyone has a double?" She made that noise again. "Only, I had one—still do maybe. She took my place here, and she said she did some things . . ."

"It was YOU. You, you bitch. YOU! You wrecked that scene in Reck's movie—and when he saw the rushes he stopped taking tranquillizers and started saying it was the funniest thing on the planet. So now he's making a movie that's a spoof of moviemaking. And we all have to LIVE our parts—and I can't even take a SHOWER or wash my HAIR for another ten DAYS. It's . . . it's . . ."

"I thought I could smell—"

"*SHUT* UP, you bitch. Or I'll . . . I'll . . ."

But she started to cry. And then she screamed and shouted at no one or everyone in the world, "No, I MUSTN'T even CRY. Mustn't SPOIL the PATTERN of the MESS on my FACE . . ."

All this while the slinko had been whizzing on, and we'd reached the studio. The car stopped. And Turquoise sat there and so did I, although the doors opened. They're automatic, the whole car is, driver included. It'd only stopped to pick me up because Reck so wanted to see me.

I began to feel really, really mean.

"Turquoise," I said, after a minute.

"What? You *beast*."

"Look, it wasn't me. But maybe—maybe this new angle'll really *help* your career—"

"This . . . looking like *this*? I can't break the contract or I'd be gone. I tell you, the minute we're done I am gone. GONE. Damn Ollywood. I am going to get a job in Dad's firm. I am going to sell robot smailers."

I said, even more quietly, "You know, Turquoise, you are so pretty—"

"Don't you lie to me, you little—"

"No, you *are* pretty—even like that—you kind of still look good . . ."

It was an utter lie. But poor old T, she just sat there, and then she turned and gazed at me. And there was the vaguest glint of hope in her eyes. "But, Jet—I *can't* do—"

"No, really. You're really beautiful, and it sort of . . . shines through. And you *don't* smell. Er, not really. Just

185

of the plastery stuff in your hair. Nothing—it's not that bad."

One last tear leaked out her turquoise eye. I'd so seldom said anything nice to her, not for years, she had to believe me.

"Oh, Jet," she said. And she leaned over and kissed me, real careful not to smudge her mess pattern. But it still left a little white mark on my cheek.

Then we'd gotten out the car and went up to today's soundstage, which was Number 113. And there in the foyer were all these other irritable and upset actors looking (and smelling) just about like Turquoise. And old Wreck-Reck (clean and scented) came flying from nowhere and sort of fell at my feet with joy. And Bronze Shunk (in much less mess than everyone else) strode over to say hi to me, but then he saw Otis and backed off with his hand clamped over his teeth.

Then Mom was there and Dad, and Amber. And after they threw their arms around me, even Amber, Dad said I must make a public apology for the trouble I'd caused.

But Reck wouldn't hear of that.

He said you couldn't confine genius. He said I must be in the new version of the movie. He wanted me to swing in on a rope or something and vanish in midair—and how did I *do* that trick?

Luckily, just before I made the mistake of trying again to explain that it hadn't been me, or Otis, Otis's two back legs fell off, and at the same moment some invading weed-guano blew up one of the Overcameras, and everyone got evacuated. Except Reck. Who stayed to film the destruction.

Reck's movie is out by now. You may have heard of it; it won twenty O'Scars. You can see it at any good cinematic, and soon it'll be on telecine. Good old Reckless Reck, the critics all say. What a risk taker. And Turquoise didn't leave Ollywood. She was offered another part right after, Second Slave to the Empress of Venusseven, in the new epic *Venus Destroyed*, directed by Tiberius Prancer. Probably be out next year.

But the rest of us came home. Even Amber.

She'd turned up the evening before we left and said she wanted to come, too. She said Reck was too old for her, he bored her silly. She said she was really sorry, because she knew how much we had all been thrilled about her dating him but she had told him they were through. He dedicated the *Fall of the Fall of Super Troy* to her anyhow. Sad. Am I going to get that sloppy when I'm old? Hope not.

As for me, I didn't start a career in movies either. Dad just marched in and told Reck I had to get back to school, and anyway I didn't know how to disappear in midair. I wasn't a member of the Professional Magicians' Senate, so forget it.

Never thought I'd be glad to get back to school. And I'm not. But better school than Reck. All the girls are envious, though, because I met him, and hey—had I *spoken* to Bronze Shunk? I said Otis had knocked one of Bronze's teeth out. Then none of them would speak to me the whole semester.

I've lost interest in those guys I liked before—Georgis, Scott. There is another guy now, next year up. He looks just a bit like a really young Aragon—or maybe I should say a really, *really* young Milsner. Wonder why I like him. Odd. But he never sees me.

Sometimes, just now and then, I do wonder . . .

I do wonder if I dreamed it all. Only I didn't. I know I

didn't. But I think about the other Jet, Jet 2. And I ask myself what she is doing, there in Indigara.

Sometimes I worry that she has caused problems in there, too. None of the other humans who went there ever left, the way I did. So their shadows stayed out here in their place. And like Ben/Theb said, they kept quiet and got day jobs.

But my shadow went the other way, and Otis's, too. And in that other world, she can be any age she wants and do anything she wants. Scary.

She said I missed my chance. She said I didn't know what I wanted, or couldn't handle what I could have had.

Maybe she was right.

I don't know that, either.

Just now and then I dream of Indigara. Nothing much, usually. Just watery or fiery music, the forest, the ocean, vines with blue grapes, a glimpse of a dragon—earth, air, fire, water. Not Aragon, or Becky. Or Theb.

Once I did dream about the war we didn't have. All the ships up on the water and clouds of fire and smoke—a pretty scary dream. But . . . just a dream.

In none of the dreams am *I* ever back there. I think I'm

just remembering. Perhaps I always will dream of Indigara. Maybe it depends how many other strange things happen in my life. If any do.

Better sleep now. Got to be up and ready for the guy who looks like young Milsner to ignore.

A couple of days before we left Studiocity, I met Ben again (shadow Ben, I guess) in the park. I'd been looking out for him in a way. I watched him awhile from a distance. Seeing how like Theb he is, obviously, but now so much thinner and older and sadder, and so different, too. Ben the shadow. You can, when you know, kind of see through him.

Weird thing. Otis made an excuse and trotted off when I went up to Ben. Embarrassed?

"Hi, Ben."

He glanced up. I wondered if he'd remember me, and if he did whether he'd know that I know he is really someplace else. If Ben knew all Theb knew, if only in some *shadowy* way.

But Ben just smiled. "Hello, Jet." And then he said, "Otis is acting more like a dog today." I looked back, and

Otis seemed to be sniffing at a tree, after a rat or something, only I knew he was pretending . . . acting.

"Right. Ben." I added, "I was worried about you after you were in that fight with Milsner in the Subway."

"That's okay. You needed to get away. I should never have let you go with me . . . But I can fight, if I have to. I used to wrestle professionally once. Well . . . I was in the movies once."

"I know. I . . . I heard."

"Those were the days. I had a wife then. Back then. And you won't believe this—she and I, we had an early model of a dog like your Otis. Not so good as your Otis. But he was . . . he was good."

"What happened?"

"Oh. The usual. I didn't get anyplace in films, and she met someone else. And when she left me, she took the dog."

It was sad. It was the true sad that's called sorrow.

In a while I said that my family and I were going home. Ben smiled again and then said he wished me luck. Then he said a thing that really startled me. Maybe it shouldn't have. "Well, I guess I'll get off down the Subway. I'm meeting Martha tonight. You ever met Martha? We're together. And no one serves coffee and doughnuts like my Martha."

And now I really do have to go to sleep. Night, Otis. Old silver fur. Best friends, Otis, forever and a day. Love you, Otis. (Look, breathing mechanism on, switched off in fake sleep . . . to make me happy.) Yeah, Otis. *Love* you.

OTIS'S DISKRIPT

My half-yearly service, when I finally went in for it, took a lot longer than normal. No surprise there.

On my return to the Latters, I felt completely myself again. I have also given up the pointless foolishness of blaming myself for any errors. They were beyond my control, not only because of the missed service, but because of the excessive amount of mechanical failures then taking place in Studiocity. Though others tend to forget, I, too, am a mechanical creature. Indigara, of course, was even worse. Indigara, in a way, is the very *spirit* of all Ollywood. The great Invented Dream.

Of course, *I* never dream.

Or, I believed I didn't. But perhaps my . . . I can find

no words but *great affection* for Jet . . . has made me gradually more open to human states. It must be that.

First of all, I have had an idea, which seems to me—rationally—quite silly. But nevertheless, my actual reasoning itself suggests it may be a possibility. It involves the dragons of Indigara. I'd been bothered that while Thebennas had his air dragon and Bekmira Ren, or Rena Kimber (her original name had been Renee Martha Kemberley), had her water dragon, Jet's dragon of fire hadn't been the one that appeared on A7. If she and I were about to get pulled into Indigara, surely the dragon we saw must have had something to do with Jet. But it seems not. It was a water dragon. I have to note here that my production date, if worked out like a human star chart, would make me a Pisces. Which is a water sign. I can't quite shake this disturbing notion that the dragon I chased in the Subway had appeared not for Jet . . . but for *me*.

Perhaps, then, to have a dream—as a human would—is not so curious, particularly because—

Last night, I dreamed I went to Indigara.

In the dream I bounded through the forest, and, reaching a high cliff above the sea, I stood and watched as night changed to midday and back to night in a matter of six minutes.

When the golden ship appeared on the water, I assumed at once it was Bekmira's. Then I was less sure.

The ship was escorted now not by water dragons but by those of fire. For every so often they rose up and breathed out bright scarlet smokes. On the deck sat a young woman with long black hair, and her eyes were black. She was about sixteen. And not so beautiful as Bekmira, though very attractive and well groomed. A dog I know well from reflective surfaces lay at her feet. He wore a spiked collar, and he growled. She was Jet. Not my Jet, the *other* Jet. The shadow Jet. Even seen at this distance there was a red gleam in her eyes. And behind her, coming in now from the horizon, sailed a great war fleet, soldiers shining on the decks, drums beating, scarlet banners flying. Warlike music played. And voices were shouting a name I strained my acute ears to catch. It was *Taljerett*.

She had said, Jet's shadow, that she and the shadow Otis would conquer the world of Indigara. It seemed to me in the dream that she was in the middle of doing that, and managing pretty well.

When I "woke up" I knew I must never tell *my* Jet about this dream. I record it here as, perhaps, a sort of warning—to someone—to *anyone* who may gain access to my diskript.

Anyone, that is, ever likely to be drawn into

INDIGARA.

Tanith Lee was born in 1947 in London, England. Though she was unable to read until almost the age of eight, she began writing at the age of nine. After school she worked as a library assistant, shop assistant, a filing clerk and a waitress. She spent one year at art college.

To date she has published almost eighty novels, thirteen short story collections and well over 250 short stories. Four of her radio plays were broadcast by the BBC and she wrote two episodes of the BBC TV cult SF series *Blake's Seven*. Firebird has published her Claidi Journals (*Wolf Tower*, *Wolf Star*, *Wolf Queen*, and *Wolf Wing*), and her picaresque novel *Piratica*.

She has twice won the World Fantasy Award for short fiction, and was awarded the August Derleth Award in 1980 for her novel *Death's Master*.

Tanith Lee lives with her husband, the writer and artist John Kaiine, on the southeast coast of England.

Her Web site is **www.tanithlee.com**